FREDDIE HAMILTON grew up in the rural southeast of Tasmania, where his family had a wildlife sanctuary. He spent his childhood making friends with unusual animals li

cou

incl

natural environment.

on to complete his post-graduate

Development Studies at Oxford University. *The Field* is his first novel.

THE
FIELD

FREDDIE
HAMILTON

The Book Guild Ltd

First published in Great Britain in 2022 by
The Book Guild
Unit E2, Airfield Business Park
Harrison Road
Market Harborough
Leicestershire, LE16 7UL
Freephone: 0800 999 2982
www.bookguild.co.uk
Email: info@bookguild.co.uk
Twitter: @bookguild

Typeset in 11pt Adobe Garamond Pro

Printed and bound by CPI Group (UK) Ltd, Croydon, CR0 4YY

ISBN 978 1914471 261

British Library Cataloguing in Publication Data.
A catalogue record for this book is available from the British Library.

For Poudge

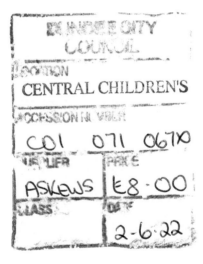

1

THE HEDGEROW

1

There was a bustle along the Hedgerow. The sun shone weakly through a crisp autumnal sky. Its rays tickled the orange and red leaves of the hawthorns and sloes, twinkling off the dew drops hovering at their tips. For the field mice of the Hedgerow, there was not a moment to spare to appreciate such things; there was lots to be done. Things to harvest and collect, things to fold and stack, things to dust and clean – all before the winter ahead.

The field mice were busy creatures. For as long as any animal in the Field could remember, it had always been that way. On warm summer evenings they sat in the uppermost branches of the Hedgerow chattering excitedly about how envious the rest of the creatures in the Field must be of them. Although proud of their modesty, an eavesdropping outsider would have been easily fooled into thinking they spoke with an air of superiority, as if they thought themselves better than the Field's other creatures. They would boast about how their queen was more beautiful and richer than the grey squirrel chief of the oak Copse in the middle of the Field. They would babble about how they collected and stored more food than the voles in the Watermeadow at the Field's edge, and how they tunnelled better than the moles in the Bottom Corner. They would chuckle about how many more words their language had and how much nicer it was to listen to than that of the Warren's busily burrowing rabbits. They would write songs about how they were wiser than the owls in the Elms along the River and how they knew more about the stars. And they would muse about how long it would be before they found a way to fly higher and faster than the starlings.

Despite this bravado, credit is needed where credit is due. The field mice had gone from a motley bunch of bandits to the Hedgerow's rulers in only a few generations. As they got better at deciding what they all wanted and protecting themselves from the other creatures who called the Hedgerow home, they took more of it as their own. Growing stronger, they invaded the final bits of the Hedgerow that were not theirs, overpowering the larger and stronger rats and forcing them to carve weapons and collect berries, nuts and sticks to build nests. Freed from these burdens, the field mice set about turning the Hedgerow into a fortress, driving the red squirrels from the upper branches and replacing them with ranks of soldiers, heavily armed with sharp wooden swords, sturdy clubs and long spears.

No longer needing to share the food the Hedgerow provided, and with more room to build nests, the number of field mice grew and grew. Before long, the Hedgerow became cramped. There was not enough food to go around and many soldiers had no weapons, the army growing faster than the rats could carve them.

The final straw for the field mice Queen came one unusually sweltering midsummer afternoon. Among the branches and thronging, always-busy field mice, the Hedgerow was unbearably stifling with little fresh air or room to lay down and relax one's paws. The Queen called a meeting with her advisors and, there and then, they agreed that the Hedgerow had become far too small. They needed more space and creatures to gather food and make weapons for them. The Field was a big place and many creatures called it home. There was only one thing to do: the field mice needed to take more of it for themselves.

2

The rabbits from the Warren next to the Hedgerow were a talkative lot, preferring to discuss how things should be done rather than doing them. Rumour had it they had once ruled the Hedgerow but no creature in the Field knew for sure, all surprised and raising their furry, feathery or scaly eyebrows whenever it was mentioned. There were two things all the creatures did know though: the rabbits were a shadow of their former selves and there was now a big network of abandoned burrows under the Field. Some creatures said the rabbits only used one burrow in ten, others one in a hundred – no creature knew for sure.

Many older field mice remembered waking on a bright spring morning in seasons past and looking out from the Hedgerow across the Field. Fountains of loam had flown up, up, up in the air, pattering gently into piles where sun-yellow buttercups and sunset-magenta thistles bloomed eagerly. These creatures also remembered how mysteriously, as if almost overnight, many younger rabbits had become ill, the earth underneath their paws shaking gently as the bunnies coughed in their beds underground. The fountains of soil then no longer came from the digging of burrows but from the digging of graves, the meadow above the Warren left covered in countless bare mounds. Watered by the salty tears of mothers and fathers, brothers and sisters, the buttercups and thistles grew no longer. The earth stayed bare, baked hard and smooth like the pebbles on the Riverbank by the summer sun.

The Field's creatures thought differently about the rabbit's demise. The grey squirrels concluded it was a miasma, the more imaginative claiming that, from the top of the oak trees in the Copse, they had seen a fine mist hovering above the entrances to the Warren. The moles from the Bottom Corner, always modest in their ambitions and bound deeply to the doctrines of a deity who made the soil smell sweet and not too moist, yet not too dry, let their superstitions run free.

'It's that there burrowin',' they claimed. ''Ent no creature 'as ev'r as burrowed s'much.' They would pause for a moment, scratching their noses thoughtfully before continuing. 'Them bin upsetting th'Lord, and as all who be a gud creature know, th'Lord... Now 'e be takin' 'is revenge!'

Looking down their snouts at the moles, the voles took a more matter-of-fact approach. 'It's all in the density,' they mused. 'So very many bunnies, it mattered not how many very deep burrows were dug, there was always going to be far too many hoppers and not enough holes.'

'That's why we have lots of tidy, separate burrows for each family along the Riverbank,' the otters agreed, ever pragmatic.

The badgers, on the other paw, wasted no effort wondering why it had happened, for they knew that, with the rabbits, it had always been the case. The number of creatures in the Warren grew and shrank and grew again, much as the River rose and fell from winter to summer. The badgers' parents had seen it, much as their great-grandparents' great-grandparents had. Seasons past or seasons to come, it was to be expected.

Unlike these creatures, the field mice showed little interest in the rabbits' troubles. They were busy. There was food to collect, swords and armour to make, and a hedgerow to keep safe from intruders.

This all changed the stifling day the Queen met with her advisors.

3

The Queen and her advisors spent a while discussing what they would do. Then, on a mild, overcast day at the very beginning of spring, after a long winter had made the field mice restless, they decided to invade the Warren while it was weak. With the Hedgerow's large army, the Queen thought it would be easy. Half the soldiers would dig a few new openings to the Warren, invading the unused tunnels and surprising the rabbits. The other half would guard the entrances, stopping the rabbits from fleeing, trapping them in their own Warren.

A field mouse, who had once spent half a dozen seasons living in an oak tree in the Copse, was quick to share the grey squirrels' thoughts about the miasma still hanging in the tunnels, waiting to catch intruders unawares. Another field mouse, whose uncle had once met a mole while exploring on a picnic, mentioned that they thought the rabbits were cursed. The Queen and her advisors paid no attention; they wanted Progress, and this required more field mice who needed more space and more food which had to be collected and stored.

The rabbits were caught by surprise. Although the field mice did not pride themselves on being violent, many creatures died. Across the Field, stories spread of the Warren's tunnels flowing with blood, darker than the juice from the bramble berries in the Thicket where the ferrets lived. And, although the field mice did not pride themselves on being courageous, for it was 'terribly old-fashioned, really', many heroes were made, their legends ingrained proudly in the memories of field mice for many seasons to come. To make sure the actions of the bravest soldiers were not forgotten, the Queen gave each hero a wooden medal carved by a rabbit who no longer looked to their tsar for guidance, but to her, although she was never seen. She stayed hidden behind rows of guards in her palace, the biggest and most beautiful field mouse-made thing in the Hedgerow. And the Tsar of the Warren? He and his family fled with strict instructions from the Queen never to return. Like all rulers in the Field, their families had known each other far longer than any creature could remember. As they left the Warren, the Tsar and his family cried cold tears of betrayal. They had lost their home.

As seasons passed, the rabbits, like the rats before them, began to speak fewer rabbit words and more field mouse words. Before long, the rabbits found themselves wearing jackets like the field mice wore and eating foods the field mice ate. Many rabbits were sad that this was happening; that, although they were still rabbits, they were becoming more like their captors. Some rabbits liked it, using it to their advantage. Putting themselves forward, they led the rabbit groups formed by the field mice to collect berries, nuts and wood, and carve weapons, getting more food and perhaps a slightly bigger nest by doing so. On the other paw, many rabbits grew very angry, forming small rebel groups and refusing to speak, eat or wear jackets like the field mice did. When the moon hung highest in the night sky, these rebels met at the end of long secret tunnels in the Warren field mouse soldiers would never find. They dreamt of the day they could truly be rabbits again, and kept some of the old rabbit ways of doing things to preserve rabbitness for when they would finally be freed from the Hedgerow. They even went as far as plotting this downfall – a glorious revolution where all rabbits would rise up against the field mice. What a dream! Some rebels were impatient and tried to start the revolution straight away. The field mice were too strong, their numbers too many. The rabbits had to wait.

The responses from the Field's other creatures to the invasion of the Warren were mixed. The moles thought it a good thing the rabbits 'were bein' sort'd out all gud'n proper' and that 'the old Tsar there, 'e be s'useless as 'is pa 'n 'is pa 'fore 'im – it were 'im that got all 'em bunnies in'o this 'ere mess'.

The voles took a different view. They were scared. 'You must look here,' they argued, 'if such a thing has been happening to the rats and the rabbits, who's to be saying that we might not be next?' Immediately they began training a small army and building forts from reeds to guard their Watermeadow – just in case.

But the field mice did not merely see their invasion of all the Hedgerow and Warren as only good for them.

'It's our duty!' the Queen began in a speech she gave every midsummer to a thronging crowd of field mice outside her palace. 'We must make them more like us! The willingness with which the rats and rabbits gave into us proves that they were unable to look after themselves. It is our duty to provide direction and guidance to those in the Field not as clever or organised as ourselves.' The crowd chattered excitedly. The Queen stopped, waiting for the hubbub to die down before resuming. 'It is our duty, and I, as your leader, am duty-bound by God to do this.' She paused for a brief moment, her words hanging in the air like an echo. 'It is God's will; they wish it to be so.'

The applause was thunderous, shaking the leaves on the Hedgerow's upper branches. Sunlight flickered gently over the crowd, dappling the furry faces like a breeze rippling the River's surface in the late summer sun.

The crowd of field mice swayed, drunk on the newfound belief that they were essential to everything in the Field. From the growing of the grass to the thawing of the frost, they felt it had something to do with them. But not a single creature stopped to inspect the golden sword brandished by the Queen to point the way. Who was God? Was the field mice's god the same as the moles' god? As the otters'? As the rats' and rabbits', even? Was it the same god, treating each of the creatures differently? Or was it a different god? A god that hid among the Hedgerow's branches rather than the boughs of the Copse? Not even the Queen had thought much about it. The rats and rabbits, who closed their eyes and whispered in the darkness to their own gods every night before they went to sleep, asking for freedom, did not think about it. The only thing all the creatures thought was that there was a god on their side, always – a god who would make everything better.

So, the field mice ploughed steadily onwards, sculpting the rats and rabbits so they were easier to control and more like them – more useful to their cause. Otherwise, apart from the voles, few creatures paid much attention to what was happening in the Hedgerow, just as the field mice had done when the rabbits were ill. There was lots to be done. Most creatures were too busy collecting food for the winter or repairing nests and burrows to worry about what such things, far away on the other side of the Field, meant for them. 'If it hasn't happened to us before, why should it happen now?' they all said.

Some of them were wrong.

4

The field mice were clever creatures, there is no doubt. Not long after invading the Warren, they realised that the rats and rabbits were collecting and storing far more food and wood than the Hedgerow needed for many seasons to come. Despite this, things for the field mice were not without problem. Winters in the Hedgerow were bitterly cold, its leafless skeleton of branches and twigs doing little to stop the biting wind whistling through.

In seasons past, most of the Field's creatures retreated to their burrows for the winter, holing themselves up snug and warm until the chill lifted. But things had changed; now there was too much to be done. The field mice could not waste a whole season snoozing; they had to be out and about supervising the rats and rabbits and guarding their hedgerow. To make matters worse, the Hedgerow had no gnarled mulberry trees like the Copse, leaving the field mice without the little silk pods that grew in their branches which the grey squirrels weaved into snug jackets and hats. And unlike the Riverbank, neither did the Hedgerow have a river full of fish and shrimp. Rich and oily, these gave the otters a thick layer of insulation around their tummies.

Instilled with a sense of adventure, field mice often left the Hedgerow, travelling the Field to learn about the other creatures and their lives. In doing so, they discovered how the grey squirrels and otters kept warm. Not only this, they also learnt a couple of other things too. Because the otters insisted on digging bigger, deeper burrows for each family, they were collecting all the wood on the Riverbank to strengthen them and keep out the winter floods. Now there was little wood left. The number of grey squirrels in the Copse was also growing, many often going hungry in winter, for there were not enough of their favourite acorns to go around.

The field mice had lots of food. Nuts and berries grew readily in the Hedgerow, and the rats and rabbits were good at collecting other things like flower bulbs and fungi too. A living thing, the Hedgerow was constantly growing around the field mice, plenty of wood falling to the ground from the hawthorns, sloes and elderflowers when it died, making it easy to collect.

Realising these things, the Queen selected a special group of intrepid ambassadors who, at one point or another, had each lived on the Riverbank or in the Copse. Lined up in front of her throne, the Queen gave them strict instructions. 'You will visit the Riverbank and Copse. Do not return until the otter elders have agreed to swap shrimp and fish for our wood, and the grey squirrel Chief silky pods for nuts and berries.' The ambassadors nodded – this was not going to be easy. 'What I am asking is very important, the lives of many creatures in the Hedgerow depend on you,' she finished curtly.

The ambassadors stared at the Queen unblinkingly. To their knowledge, no creature in the Field had ever been asked to do something like this before.

The next morning, they set out from the Hedgerow, crunching through a blanket of frost towards the Riverbank.

5

The otters were stern, thoughtful creatures but friendly enough. Arriving at the Riverbank, tired and dishevelled from their long journey, the ambassadors' first challenge was simply talking to their hosts – Otter was a peculiar language, baring little resemblance to Field Mouse. The Queen and her advisors had given little thought to this, so the ambassadors decided to stay a while to tackle the tough, tongue-tangling words. This played into their paws. Just as they were beginning to chat properly with the otters, the autumn rains came.

And came they did, with greater intensity than any otter could remember. The River rose quickly, turning into an oozing, muddy soup. Soon the waters were rushing up against the entrance of the otters' burrows, threatening to break in. The otters were scared; the ambassadors could tell.

One morning, the ambassadors woke to learn that three families had been washed away in the middle of the night and they seized their chance. As best they could, for their Otter was still fairly basic, the ambassadors explained that, if the otters took a little wood from the Hedgerow, this sad situation might not happen again. Narrowing their eyes and wrinkling their noses, the otter elders wondered why the field mice were offering this. What did they want in return? They soon found out, the ambassadors adding that the field mice would happily swap their wood for the same amount of fish and shrimp.

The otters had never seen the Riverbank as just somewhere they lived. They saw it as part of them; an important part that provided all the things they needed and kept them safe. While not as devout as the moles, the otters believed that the soil they stood on, the River they swam in, the fish and shrimp they ate, and the sky above, were all separate gods. As tempting as the ambassadors' offer was, it forced the elders to stop and think. There had always been enough fish and shrimp in the River; what would happen if they caught more than before? Up until recently, the god of plants had always provided enough wood and the elders were mindful of upsetting them by taking more from somewhere else. They knew gods sometimes got angry when the otters did something they did not like. Maybe using more wood than they should have was the reason for these floods? If they caught more fish and shrimp, would this upset the River god? If so, what would the god do?

The ambassadors were impatient to leave the Riverbank. They had been with the otters for quite a while and much preferred the Hedgerow's dry branches to the Riverbank's damp burrows. They still had to visit the grey squirrels too, and this made them anxious. The grey squirrels had a reputation for being difficult to get along with. Finally, the otter elders told the ambassadors that they would have a meeting to discuss their offer properly. The ambassadors waited.

While this was happening, the River kept rising to heights not even the oldest otter could recall. Burrow after burrow flooded and many old, sick and baby otters were carried away, still sleeping in their beds, never to be seen again. Some otters abandoned their dry stoicism, becoming hysterical and superstitious. As more otters got swept away, these thoughts spread like an infection. The number of crying brothers, wailing sisters, screaming mothers and yelling fathers outside the biggest burrow grew and the elders felt the otters' trust in them fading. If they could not solve this problem, would they still be wanted? Would they still be needed?

Worried and tired from sleepless nights of discussion, the elders finally gave in. Dipping his paw in mulberry juice ink, the eldest elder pressed it next to the Queen's dainty print on an agreement scratched in curly shapes on a dried chestnut leaf. As soon as the ink dried, the leaf was rolled up, slipped into a hollow of birchwood and tied around the neck of a wiry field mouse messenger who had accompanied the ambassadors. With a nod of thanks and couple of skips to stretch his hind paws, the messenger was off, bounding from stone to stone along the Riverbank towards the Hedgerow and the waiting Queen.

This was a momentous moment for both the otters and field mice. The carefully scratched shapes on the chestnut leaf explained how the Hedgerow would swap wood with the Riverbank for the same amount of fish and shrimp. Being so far from the Riverbank, the ambassadors devised a clever way to dry the fish and shrimp in the sun, making them easy to carry and stopping them from going bad on the long journey to the Hedgerow. The otters had never done this before. They had no need to carry and store their fish and shrimp, they could catch and eat them straight from the River.

Happy, albeit with sniffly noses and chesty coughs from the damp, the ambassadors left the Riverbank. The agreement was an important thing for the Field, both the otters and field mice knew that. Never before had two groups of creatures swapped things they needed but did not have for things they had but did not need. When they heard, the moles, voles and shrews all claimed that they had thought of it before, and maybe they had. But the Hedgerow and Riverbank's agreement was for swapping previously unthinkable: wood for dried fish and shrimp, something to build burrows with for something to eat. This was far more than a pawful of nuts or berries here and there.

The otters could hardly believe it. They felt duped; forced into a corner and drugged by a heady cocktail of field mouse cunning. But consolation came quickly. As the exhausted messenger placed the agreement in her paw, the Queen ordered the first loads of wood to be taken to the Riverbank. The Hedgerow had to wait; its first supply of fish and shrimp could not happen until the late spring when the sun's rays were strong enough to dry them. This was a big risk for the field mice; much could happen in a season or two. Maybe the otter elders would change their minds? But no, the elders knew of the size and strength of the Hedgerow's army. This was all the Queen needed to make sure the otters kept to the agreement – they would never think of doing otherwise.

6

eaving the Riverbank, the ambassadors hurried towards the Copse to visit the grey squirrels. The Field over, the grey squirrels were renowned as a stubborn bunch, led by a chief with a reputation for being erratic. Many stories about him abounded, including a rumour that he ate the flesh of his enemies after hanging them by their tails from the highest branch of the Copse's tallest oak tree for a whole moon cycle.

There was a sense of urgency among the ambassadors. The cold, wet winter meant the field mice needed silky pods to weave snug jackets and hats to keep them warm and dry straight away. There was no going back to the Hedgerow with empty paws. To add to their worries, the Copse had a strong army too. Although not as big as the Hedgerow's, the fear the ambassadors had relied upon negotiating with the otters would work no longer. They needed to use cunninger tactics, which they thought up on the journey from the Riverbank to the Copse.

The ambassadors had no chance to use these plans,

though. Unexpectedly, upon their arrival in the Copse, grey squirrel soldiers were waiting for them and knew why they were there. The ambassadors were puzzled; this had been a top-secret visit, unknown to any creature other than the ambassadors, the Queen and her closest advisors. Unlike the otters, the grey squirrels were not renowned for their hospitality and the ambassadors were not welcomed with open forepaws. Grabbed roughly, the ambassadors were dragged by burly grey squirrel soldiers to a heavily guarded hollow in an old oak in the middle of the Copse. Here they were kept for many days without food or water. Asking why they were being held, the ambassadors were poked viciously in response with long spears. From underneath their walnut shell helmets the guards spat out venomously, 'The Chief be very busy n'youse lot'll jus 'ave t'wait, oright?' The days passed in misery for the poor ambassadors, the joy they felt from the agreement with the otters rapidly replaced by helplessness and despair.

Grey Squirrel and Field Mouse were similar languages, and the ambassadors thought this would work in their favour negotiating with the inhabitants of the Copse, but it turned out to have the opposite effect. Although they no longer had the same difficulty talking to their hosts as they had experienced with the otters, the ambassadors were unable to discuss things in secrecy and plan an escape. What a pickle the ambassadors found themselves in!

One morning, as the sun peeked over the wintry horizon, causing the Field's frosted grass to glint and sparkle with many colours of the rainbow all at once, the ambassadors were poked rudely awake with spears. Grasped by four grey squirrel soldiers apiece, the ambassadors were dragged, shivering with cold and trembling with fear, to finally meet the Chief. The biggest and strongest of all grey squirrels, with the downiest coat, bushiest tale and pointiest ears, the Chief sat in a large hollow in the Copse's tallest oak tree. His voice matched his size, booming around the hollow, bouncing off knots and grooves in the walls and ceiling. 'I know why you field mice are here: you think that we in the Copse are hungry.' He spoke slowly and with much consideration. He paused, his eyes the milky darkness of a cloudless night in the low light. 'You wish to swap food for our silky pods to make jackets for the freezing creatures in the Hedgerow.'

His voice was stern and the ambassadors could tell he was insulted that the field mice had noticed that there was not enough food in the Copse and wanted to take advantage of it. He paused again thoughtfully before resuming, slightly louder than before. 'You field mice are wrong! The Copse is strong and we need no more food – especially not from dirty field mice!' He spat the last words with contempt. 'Your food is not fit for noble grey squirrels!' Finishing, the Chief rose from his throne to his full imposing height, a staff set with small, shining stones in his paw.

The ambassadors knew that he was not speaking truthfully. On their travels, the field mice found out much about the other creatures and what they did, including many things these creatures would have preferred them not to know. At the end of the previous spring, one such traveller had found himself hiding in a shadowy corner of the very same chamber the ambassadors now cowered in. Seated in his throne, the traveller had seen the Chief become angry when his advisors told him there were not enough acorns to feed all the creatures in the Copse. Pressing them on what should be done for the coming winter, the Chief had become frustrated when the advisors had no answers. Hearing this conversation and seeing grey squirrels squabbling over the last of the autumn acorn collection, the traveller had hurriedly returned to the Hedgerow to share the news with the Queen.

The ambassadors remained silent as the Chief started towards them, nestling deeper on their hind paws and bowing their heads to escape the dull, black stare. 'We will not cooperate with field mice!' the Chief spat. 'We know what you have done to the rats and rabbits. Who's to say you will not do the same to us?' He paused once more (creatures like the Chief generally had a lot of experience getting the biggest impact from their words and presence). 'What's more,' he started again in the same spiteful tone, 'we are insulted that you think we would ever need your help. We can look after ourselves and will never forget this outrage.' The Chief sighed a long sigh. 'We are proud of who we are; a pride shaped by never forgetting the wrongs of our enemies!' His black button nose pinched and his glossy brow furrowed. 'We will not cooperate with the field mice. Not now. Not ever!'

Finishing, he drew a sharp breath and returned to his throne, resting his chin on a paw and surveying the chamber and the four ambassadors before him thoughtfully. The silence was long. Finally, he gestured to the soldiers standing by the hollow's entrance and they stepped forward briskly, grasping each ambassador by the ruff with their strong paws and dragging them out of the hollow. Up the tree they went, higher and higher, bumping over knots and being grazed by the rough bark until they arrived at the highest branch of the Copse's tallest oak. The Field spread out below the ambassadors like a map. In the distance they saw the River, still swollen and angry, and the Hedgerow, peaceful in the gentle morning light. A little closer to the Copse, they saw the moles' hills, arranged in a higgledy-piggledy fashion in the Bottom Corner. Behind that, over near the Great Elm, they saw the entrances to the badgers' Sett: mysterious, dark holes among the roots. Laying on the branch, teeth chattering with cold and fear, the ambassadors cared little for the view.

Suddenly, with a squeal of surprise, the eldest ambassador's tail was grabbed and he was hoisted up, behind first. Were the rumours true? The ambassadors thought suddenly. Were they going to be hung by their tails for a whole moon cycle? With a couple more quick actions, two more ambassadors joined the first, their tails knotted over a stout twig. Sagging under the new weight, the twig bounced gently with their quiet sobs. Like his friends, the tail of the final and youngest ambassador was grabbed but, to his surprise, instead of it being looped around the twig, he was dragged back down the tree. Unsure whether to be frightened of what lay ahead or relieved at being spared the end of his friends, he sobbed.

It was not long until the soldiers and the youngest ambassador reached the bottom bough of the tallest oak. Wordlessly, the grip on his tail was released and nature took over. Head over hind paw, the youngest ambassador tumbled the last few yards to the ground, landing with a bump and a thud in the musty, damp leaves. Dazed, he hurried upright, glancing about in confusion. Without choosing a direction, he fled through the Copse away from the biggest oak, in a direction he hoped was towards the Hedgerow. As he did so, the youngest ambassador heard laughter from the branches of the trees above mingling with the cries of rooks. Glancing upwards as he ran, he thought he saw beady, black grey squirrel eyes staring down from the canopy. Behind him, the rooks whirled on the gentle morning breeze about the top of the tallest oak. As he looked upwards, the youngest ambassador tripped on a root hidden in the leaves and fell flat on his snout. He lay for a moment panting heavily before hurrying upright, fear and blood rushing through his veins like a field mouse mother frantically looking for a lost pup. Taking off again, he ran faster than he had ever thought of running before, looking nowhere but straight ahead.

Away – away from the tallest oak, away from the grey squirrels, away from his friends squirming upside down and away from the cawing rooks. Home – home towards the safety of the Hedgerow. The youngest ambassador hoped with all his pounding heart that the Queen would believe his tale. If not, a fate worse than that of the other ambassadors might await.

7

The youngest ambassador was shaken, exhausted and lucky. Upon his return to the Hedgerow, he was ushered straight into the Queen's chamber where he cowered on his hind paws before the throne. While the mulberry leaf agreement with the otters had arrived quickly back from the Riverbank, there were no congratulations. Instead, the youngest ambassador was made to recite the sorry tale, beginning from the ambassadors' arrival in the Copse. Spilling from between the ambassador's chattering teeth, the tale was slow to be told and often difficult for the eager ears of the audience to hear through the sobs. After he finished, the Queen dismissed the ambassador and he was escorted back to his eagerly awaiting family.

Following the ambassador's departure, the Queen ordered that the doors to her great chamber be closed and gave the guards strict instructions that she and her advisors were not to be disturbed while they discussed what to do next. She was insulted by what the Chief had done to her representatives, so much so, the urgency to get soft silky pods to make jackets to stem the horrid winter chill fell by the wayside. The Queen stood her ground; the Chief had blown his chance to negotiate. In her eyes, there was now only one option: invasion.

Due to the size and skill of the Hedgerow's army, the Queen was confident with her choice. Now the rats and rabbits did most of the rummaging and foraging in the Hedgerow, the field mice were free to do things the Queen and her advisors felt more fitting for a field mouse, like being a soldier in the Field's biggest and most skilful army. Although the army was mainly for keeping enemies out of the Hedgerow, as the invasion of the Warren showed, it could attack too.

Having far more food and wood than it now needed, the Queen thought each of the soldiers in the Hedgerow's army should be given things in return for the soldiering they did. As is often the case, the Queen believed skilful soldiers were more valuable to the Hedgerow, deserving more things than those who were clumsy with a sword or could not throw a spear as far. Quickly, the army changed, with those soldiers who were stronger or more experienced getting more food and wood to build nests than younger, weaker soldiers.

Rewarding the soldiers worked well, improving the army's organisation as better, stronger soldiers were put in charge of those who were weaker: those given more things now above those given less. The soldiers' families changed as well, the children of the soldiers rewarded with more food becoming stronger and healthier than those given less. These families had more wood too, so they were able to build bigger nests. Stronger soldiers also ordered weaker ones to move their families when they wanted to live where they did. The area around the Queen's palace, where most important things in the Hedgerow happened, steadily filled with the families of the strongest soldiers. The families of the weaker soldiers now had to build their nests further from the palace and their family and friends. This made it further to carry the food and wood they were rewarded with for soldiering the afternoon before a full moon in front of the palace.

With the rats and rabbits doing most of the foraging and rummaging, the army was able to practise soldiering and defend the Hedgerow every moment of the day. In other areas of the Field, armies had to collect their own food and wood, practise soldiering and defend themselves all at once. Now spending their days only doing army things, the field mouse soldiers were ready when the Queen decided to invade the Copse, the army generals rousing them from their nests and sentry posts and marching them across the Field at the double. Being able to do this quickly gave the field mice the much-prized element of surprise. But the fate of the ambassadors had proven the grey squirrel Chief had ears within the walls of the Queen's palace.

Dawn broke the day following the youngest ambassador's return. The sun's rays tried feebly to push through the screen of drizzle hanging from the sky like a soggy, grey blanket. The entire field mice army, all except for a few left to defend the Hedgerow, squelched their way across the Field towards the Copse. All day they marched. After a quick supper as the sun took a last blink before laying its head down behind the distant Rise at the edge of the Field, the army continued silently through the sooty evening drizzle. Grey squirrel sentries watching from the oaks at the edge of the Copse saw and heard nothing. The clouds and drizzle selfishly kept the moon, stars and all the precious, faint noises of the night for themselves.

Before dawn the following day, the Hedgerow's army stopped short of the edge of the Copse. In a shallow ditch with a thin stream of water gurgling down the middle, the soldiers munched a few berries and nuts and slurped some water. Resting once more, they waited for the sky to brighten.

As the first glimmers of dawn peeked carefully through the persistent drizzle, the field mouse soldiers charged out of the ditch, swarming the Copse. Just as good at climbing as grey squirrels, they clambered up each and every oak tree, outnumbering the Copse's soldiers two score to one. Before the sun was even halfway towards its home in the middle of the sky, the field mice were done. The grey squirrels were captured, the Chief beheaded and the Queen of the Hedgerow now Empress of the Copse as well.

8

The field mice had conquered the Copse and the Chief was gone but still fighting continued for a few seasons more. Led by small bands of unruly grey squirrels, much like the rebellious rabbits from the Warren, these fighters wanted to just be grey squirrels in charge of their own whimsies, not ruled by the field mice. Many former soldiers in the Chief's army, these fighters bombarded field mice soldiers patrolling the Copse, catching them unawares. The Queen and her advisors simply hoped the rebels would tire when they realised that they were having little success. But this did not happen and the skirmishes became more frequent and intense, the bands of rebels larger. When news of a particularly bloody ambush made its way back to the Hedgerow, the Queen's oldest, wisest advisor had a clever idea to bring the rebels into line. Instead of taking the Copse away from the grey squirrels, the advisor suggested that it be divided into smaller bits with each given to close friends of the former Chief to rule themselves if they gave their support to the new Empress. So all the grey squirrels knew these new leaders had the power to rule on her behalf, the Queen gave them their own title, rajah, something the Chief would never have done.

Only thinking she was the representative of god and not one herself, the Queen could not be both in the Hedgerow and Copse at once, so she appointed a representative to oversee the Copse and keep the rajahs in line. Trusting few other creatures and wanting to protect her rule there, the Queen chose her eldest son, the Prince, who became Governor of the Copse. 'The most important thing is to make sure those pesky rajahs behave themselves and keep order in the bits of the Copse we have given them,' the Queen instructed before sending the Governor Prince away from the Hedgerow.

In addition to appointing a governor, the Queen thought the youngest and last ambassador, being experienced in both swapping and dealing with the grey squirrels, would be best to lead an important new group. With help from the Hedgerow's army, this group was unlike anything seen in the Field before, carrying out the fated ambassadors' original task of making sure as many silky pods as possible made their way from the Copse to the Hedgerow.

Upon hearing this, the other creatures in the Field knew the Hedgerow's invasion of the Copse had not just been revenge. The Queen wanted other things and, with the strongest army, little could be done to stop her. Some creatures, like the moles, scared by this, worried about the day the field mice might come and take their precious things away. Others, like the shrews (who really were very shrewd) saw an opportunity. 'Maybe we can swap something for those silky pods the field mice now have from the Copse? We could have lovely snug cloth to wrap ourselves in winter, just like them!' they would chatter excitedly.

Little did they know, it would not be long.

9

Comparing the ease of signing the agreement with the otters to the capture of the Warren and Copse, the Queen saw that using her army to take over areas of the Field was a far more difficult way of getting all the things the Hedgerow needed. If the field mice kept doing this, she thought, it would not be long before the other creatures banded together and retaliated. Although the Hedgerow's army was strong, the Queen certainly did not want to fight the badgers…

On the other paw, as well as giving the field mice a feared reputation the field over, the invasion of the Copse meant the Hedgerow now controlled the swapping of silky pods, making sure it always favoured the field mice. Like that with the otters, the swapping agreement between the Hedgerow and Copse was scrawled in curly shapes on a dried chestnut leaf, and the pawprints of the Queen and rajahs glistened brightly alongside one another at the bottom. The rajahs only had their title and ruled their own little bit of the Copse because of the field mice, so there was no negotiation. They agreed to all the things the Queen wanted.

For as long as the grey squirrels could remember, they had scampered from branch to branch in the gnarled mulberry trees that grew between the tall oaks in the Copse cheerfully collecting silky pods. After they had as many as they could carry, they would take them to one of the small streams that trickled through the Copse to scrub and stamp on them with their hind paws. Following a lot of scrubbing and stamping, the pods became a big bundle of silky, wet softness, which they then spread out on the stream's rocky bank to dry before carrying it up the tall oak trunks to their hollows. Winter afternoons were then whiled away spinning, weaving and stitching the silky bundles into snug hats and jackets to keep out the bitter chill.

The Queen wanted this to change. After much discussion with her advisors, it was agreed that the grey squirrels would only be allowed to collect the silky pods and banned from washing, stamping, spinning and weaving them into cloth for their own hats and jackets. Instead, these things would be done in the Hedgerow by the field mice. As the number of creatures in the Hedgerow continued to grow, the Queen realised that, by already having a big army and lots of rats and rabbits to do all the rummaging and foraging, field mice in seasons to come would have little to do. Although they would be able to chatter more with their families and sing and dance with their friends, they could not do this all day, every day. They needed something to do to make them useful, the Queen thought. Something to keep them busy and give the Hedgerow more to swap; something to make sure the field mice became the envy of all creatures in the Field. What better thing for them to do than weave beautiful cloth? Like their army, this was something the field mice could take pride in and be renowned for the Field over. With the winter chill affecting all the Field's creatures, they all wanted silky cloth to make jackets and hats to keep warm, and were more than willing to swap things for it.

As planned, the youngest ambassador's group took control of collecting the silky pods with help from the Hedgerow's army and, in this way, was able to get his revenge. Using the soldiers at his disposal, he forced the grey squirrels to pluck pods from the bendy branches of the mulberry trees and lug them across the Field. Too old or too slow to nimbly spring from twig to twig nabbing the delicate silky pods from where they hung between the leaves, the luggers bore the youngest ambassador's wrath as he gleefully encouraged soldiers to crack slender willow whips on their backs to hurry them on. Arriving at the other side of the Field, the exhausted luggers took the silky bundles down into the Warren where they were stacked in the rabbits' old burrows until the field mice needed them for washing and weaving.

Spending most of their days collecting silky pods, the grey squirrels had few moments spare to collect food. So, in return for the silky pods, the Queen gave the rajahs berries and nuts from the Hedgerow to feed the hungry mouths of the creatures in their bit of the Copse. By giving the rajahs food and making them responsible for giving it out, she thought it would allow the rest of the grey squirrels to toil away getting as many silky pods to the Hedgerow as they could. Lo and behold, this idea worked well, although not to the benefit of the grey squirrels, who spent all day every day collecting and lugging. Instead, the rajahs used the food as a reward, not providing every creature with the same amount. Giving some grey squirrels less food but promising them more, the rajahs were able to make them do things for them, like carve fine hollows into oak trunks. The rajahs' hollows grew and grew as this arrangement worked well, becoming the only way some creatures in the Copse could get food. Soon they became palaces like the Queen's, something the Chief had never had.

Seasons passed and a constant stream of silky pods went from the Copse to the Hedgerow. The grey squirrels grew angrier, forced to do what the field mice and rajahs wanted them to and no longer free to do as they pleased. Once again, the Queen had the upper paw. Putting the rajahs in charge of feeding the Copse's hungry mouths was a good way to control the angry grey squirrels who often turned on the field mice soldiers guarding them as they picked pods. The rajahs made their own small armies, choosing the biggest, strongest grey squirrels and asking the Governor Prince to release these squirrels from collecting and lugging silky pods. Now free to become soldiers, much like those in the Hedgerow's army, the rajah gave these grey squirrels extra food for their soldiering and loyalty. These little armies kept the other rebellious grey squirrels in check and gave the rajahs more power, so much so, among most grey squirrels, the thought of rising up against the field mice became a distant one indeed.

By banning the grey squirrels from washing, stamping, spinning and weaving the silky pods, the Hedgerow had control of something all creatures in the Field wanted but did not have. The Queen liked this very much. It was now not just the otters who wanted to swap things with the Hedgerow. Although they did not have enough cloth to swap now, when it came to making swapping agreements, the field mice would be able to make them very favourable for themselves in seasons to come.

There was one problem with this grand plan, though: the grey squirrels had been weaving silky pods into beautiful shimmering cloth for as long as they could remember and the field mice had only just started. The cloth from the Hedgerow neither had the feel like cool, flowing water or frost-like sparkle of that the grey squirrels had made. Not only this, it also took the field mice far longer to weave the same amount of cloth, and the types they weaved, with their different patterns and colours, were far fewer. The field mice got better at spinning and weaving but, not wanting to take advice from the grey squirrels and having to teach themselves, it was slow. Banned from weaving, something the Queen decreed punishable by death, the grey squirrels forgot their special cloth-making skills as the Hedgerow took over.

There was even further insult still for the grey squirrels, as the field mice swapped their cloth back to the Copse for even more silky pods. Angrily realising this, the grey squirrels had no choice; they could do nothing against the field mice and the treacherous rajahs to save their pride. Spending most of their day collecting and lugging silky pods, the grey squirrels were no longer able to forage for food, making them completely reliant upon the berries and nuts collected by the rats and rabbits in the Hedgerow and given to the rajahs by the Queen.

Many grey squirrels still whispered to one another about rising up against the rajahs and reclaiming their dignity, but these dreams only every stayed as that. The ever-present armies of the Hedgerow and the rajahs kept everything in check, spreading fear among all in the Copse.

10

While the field mice were not good at washing, stamping, spinning and weaving the silky pods into cloth, they, and the rajahs, were very good at making the grey squirrels collect and lug the pods across the Field. The piles of silky pods in the Warren quickly grew and, after a while, the field mice did start to get better at spinning and weaving, and the cloth became softer and more colourful. Soon, they also began to find simple ways which made the washing faster and helped them weave far more interesting patterns than the grey squirrels had ever managed. The field mice applied themselves spectacularly, toiling through the day and well into the evening, the stars winking at them through the Hedgerow's branches like beady eyes in the faceless night sky. It was not long before they were weaving far more cloth than both the Hedgerow and Copse needed. Now the moment had arrived and the Queen put the final part of her grand plan into action. Small groups of ambassadors, just like those which had visited the Riverbank and Copse not so long ago, travelled to other areas of the Field to find out what the creatures there would be willing to swap for the Hedgerow's new silky cloth.

The voles in the Watermeadow were first. Seeing the long pastel jackets flowing from the ambassador's shoulders, they excitedly decided to swap the blood-coloured stones found along the banks of the bubbling streams flowing into the Watermeadow, which they treasured. This was not enough for the greedy ambassadors. 'Our cloth is very special,' they responded smugly. 'We have to lug silky pods all the way across the Field to make it. You'll need to give us more than some silly old stones to get some!'

Taken aback, the vole counsellors huddled around their Sultan's throne, nattering in hushed tones for several long moments. Eventually, they parted, revealing the Sultan sitting cross-pawed in all his splendour. In his charming sing-song voice he announced: 'Of the most pungent herbs that sprout so happily from the edge of the Watermeadow where the gentle water tickles the grass, we will also give you an equal amount as you give us of your very special cloth.'

The ambassadors were fibbing; they did not think they were 'silly stones' as they told the voles; never before had they seen anything as beautiful. The stones glinted like the first star in the night sky, shining with the radiance of all the sunsets the ambassadors had seen and would ever see. Nor had the ambassadors tasted such herbs before. Leaves of this, sprigs of that; all which made their mouths burn, tingle and fizz all at once. These herbs would make all food, even the musty remnants of last winter's stores, more exciting than anything the field mice had put in their mouths before. Taken with these exotic things, and knowing the huge stores of cloth in the Warren, the ambassadors nodded their heads in agreement. The dried chestnut leaf and mulberry ink emerged from a hollow of birchwood hidden in the folds of a jacket. Dipping his paw in the ink, the Sultan pressed it next to the Queen's. The agreement was rolled away and the ambassadors bowed their way out of the chamber. Skipping away from the Watermeadow towards their next visit, the ambassadors chuckled happily, slapping one another on the back and bragging about how good they were at this new swapping thing. A messenger was dispatched immediately, taking the agreement and some of the stones and herbs back to the Hedgerow. The Queen was very pleased, giggling with glee when they were placed in her paws.

Next were the shrews in the Backwater. Unlike the voles, the shrews saw the ambassadors' sumptuous robes and, without even thinking what they could offer in return, agreed to everything immediately, which was most unlike them. Over the coming moons, the shrews assembled a collection of their finest treasures for the ambassadors to see. While this was happening, the ambassadors enjoyed themselves immensely, taking advantage of the Backwater's finest hospitality. Eventually, an impressive collection of juicy, fragrant fruits and gnarled golden nuggets were presented to them. Attracted by the fruits' dripping, sweet juices and the nuggets' gleam, the ambassadors agreed immediately too. Like the vole Sultan, the Crown Prince of the Shrews carefully dipped his paw in the mulberry juice ink and pressed it on the dried chestnut leaf next to the Queen's. Once again, the agreement was rolled up and a few fruits and golden nuggets were rushed back to the elated Queen. Her plan was working.

Drunk on their success, the ambassadors continued. Around the Field from area to area, they visited each in turn, offering creatures exquisite cloth to make hats and jackets if they swapped things the ambassadors thought special. Presented with a wonderful array of curious foods, stones and woods, the ambassadors were marvelled by things they had neither seen, tasted, sniffed nor dreamt of before.

The final visit was to the Bottom Corner. The moles had never seen cloth before, let alone worn, hung or wrapped things in it ('for 'em things be gettin' awful grubby under this 'ere ground!'), and, up until now, never fancied they would. Nonetheless, like all the other creatures, the moles gave in easily to the ambassadors, agreeing to swap some of the precious nutty fungi they found digging their burrows. They did not need the cloth; it was quite snug underground away from the frost and it would just get dirty. Their beady mole eyes could not see nearly as well as those of other creatures either, and there was no light underground for the cloth to shimmer in. What was the point? But they wanted it nonetheless. They had heard rumours that all the other creatures in the Field had it and they certainly did not want to be left out.

The ambassadors returned to the Hedgerow exhausted. They had been all the way around the Field and spent quite a few seasons away from home. On their return, they were proud to see the swapping had started, lots of lovely silky cloth leaving the Hedgerow, carried and dragged across the Field to its many new homes. Even more excitingly, coming back were the many glorious things it was being swapped for. The Queen, her advisors, the ambassadors, and all the field mice in the Hedgerow, were elated. All the Field's creatures now knew of Hedgerow and the cleverness of the field mice, who thought they were very important indeed. To them, this was happiness.

Such was the desire among all the Field's creatures to have as much silky cloth as they could, the Queen quickly built up a fine hoard of precious stones and golden nuggets. Her advisors, worried they would be stolen, tried to convince her that they should be hidden away deep in the Warren, heavily guarded by soldiers. The Queen found this very dull; she wanted all creatures to see their beauty and realise how powerful the Hedgerow had become. At her direction, the walls of her palace were covered top to bottom with the stones and nuggets, making it by far the Field's most spectacular nest, burrow or hollow. Word of its magnificence quickly spread, and creatures came from far and wide to see it, many other leaders growing envious. As more and more precious stones and nuggets made their way to the Hedgerow – far more than could ever fit on or in the palace – the Queen ordered other burrows and nests to be decorated too, along with soldier's jackets, swords, spears and shields.

While this was happening, the field mice gorged themselves on the exotic new foods arriving from all over the Field, replacing the bland berries and nuts they had always eaten. Needing a reason for why something in the Hedgerow was not the very best in the Field, the Queen blamed the rats and rabbits. 'They really are no good at collecting and storing our Hedgerow foods,' she complained. 'If not for them, we would have no need to swap our cloth for food from other creatures.' Still, rummaging and foraging was not something the field mice wanted to do themselves. They preferred sitting behind their looms, weaving shimmery cloth, gorging themselves on sweet nuts and fruits, and trying to outdo one another on the decoration of their nests with precious stones and nuggets.

Never being content to simply settle for what they had, the field mice toiled away, weaving more cloth, which meant more swapping and more yummy food, precious stones and nuggets for the Hedgerow. With evermore delicious food arriving, and having concluded the rats and rabbits were lousy at foraging for it, the Queen thought it far more important that they collect wood and carve swords, spears and all the intricate little bits of the Hedgerow's fancy new weaving looms instead. Eventually, one sunny day when the Queen was feeling particularly proud of what the Hedgerow had become, she ordered the rats and rabbits to stop foraging for food altogether. Weaving and swapping cloth was far easier and more exciting than collecting food. In doing so, the field mice became the first creatures in the Field to become completely reliant upon others to feed them.

For a few seasons after this happened, a serene and unmemorable peace descended on the Field. Very few creatures realised it, and those who did barely stopped to think why it was. Some thought it was because they had all grown so fond of the lovely silky cloth, yet all those except the field mice had no way of making it themselves. Spending all waking moments catching, picking, collecting and digging to get enough things to swap for it, these creatures joked that the peace was no surprise; no creature had the chance to think about or do anything else. Other creatures thought it was because many were scared of the Hedgerow's army. After what had happened to the Copse and Warren, it was no wonder that there was a peace: no creature would dare to kick up a fuss. Whatever the reason, during this peace some clever field mice, at the direction of the Queen herself, invented a new type of loom. Able to weave silky cloth faster than before, fewer field mice were needed to use one so the same number of creatures were able to use many more looms, weaving far more cloth.

Although the Hedgerow depended upon other creatures for food, because of the special peace, the field mice did not see it as a problem in the slightest. In fact, the very thought that this new arrangement, where each group of creatures did what they did best, swapping the things they had the most of, would fail, was remote. So remote, neither the Queen, her cleverest advisors nor any of the Field's other leaders had given it the slightest thought.

11

The field mice were not the only cunning creatures in the Field. As the peace went on, many other leaders saw that swapping things between one another seemed to work quite well – if you had something to swap. The Hedgerow was the finest example of this, seen from all over the Field as it became weighed down with precious stones and golden nuggets, its gilded branches glinting and sagging under the load. And just like their Hedgerow, the field mice began to sag as well. Sitting at their looms all day, their new diet of sweet fruits, oily fish and rich fungi made them lazy, their furry bellies protruding from beneath evermore colourful silky jackets.

The other creatures saw this delightful excess and wanted to be just like the field mice. No creatures had ever lived in such splendour or had a life so easy! In the Hedgerow, the voles, shrews, otters, and all the other creatures in the Field, thought they saw a vision of how life should be; a vision that relied on nothing more than swapping some things for other things.

Dreaming their area could one day become like the Hedgerow, the other creatures started to swap things among themselves as well. Soon it started to look a little like this: the voles swapped herbs and red stones for cloth with the field mice, red stones for fungi with the moles, and herbs for berries with the shrews. The badgers swapped nuts for cloth with the field mice, worms for dried fish with the otters and beetles for dragonflies with the stoats, and so on and so on. Before long, swapping in the Field came to resemble something like a complicated spider's web. None of the creatures, not even the field mice, had any real idea of what was coming from there and going elsewhere, or what was going from somewhere and coming here.

Jealous creatures, this annoyed the field mice. With other areas swapping with one another, they were not the only ones doing it. They had thought of it, it was their idea, but no longer were they the most important part of it. Gradually the herbs from the voles became a little stale, the dried fish from the otters a little crumbly and the golden nuggets from the shrews a little less gleaming. In return, the field mice stopped sending as much cloth or started sending some not as soft or shimmery. Doing so to protect their pride, the stores of cloth in the Warren steadily filled burrow after burrow and the field mice got a little hungrier. The other creatures, now swapping food with one another, were no longer able to give as much to the Hedgerow as before.

At this point, the special peace slowly began to drift away like a mist shooed by the sun on a winter's morning. Many creatures realised swapping things backwards and forwards did not benefit all of them the same. For some it was good and for others it was not. Most creatures thought they should only swap things they had lots of or were the very best at making. If this happened, they agreed, all creatures would benefit equally from the things they had the most of and were best at doing. In practice, this was only partly true.

The rats and rabbits were forced by the field mice to collect wood and carve swords, spears and intricate bits for the looms. Most creatures had forgotten, but, before the rats' part of the Hedgerow had been invaded by the field mice all those seasons ago, they had been the best at weaving grasses and reeds. Passed down through as many generations as there were thorns in the Hedgerow, the rats had known which grasses grew where, which were the best for baskets, which the best for nests and which made excellent hats for keeping ears dry when it rained. Likewise, before the Warren had been invaded, the rabbits had been the best at digging for roots; some they used for food and others they tore into strips to line their burrows to keep them warm. Things had changed. Now the rats and rabbits only did things the field mice wanted them to and nothing else. Almost overnight, these old skills disappeared, no longer used or even thought of.

It was the same for the grey squirrels. The best at spinning and weaving the silky pods into the finest cloth, the field mice had stopped them doing this. Now they could only collect the pods and lug them across the Field to the new looms in the Hedgerow. The moles too, yet less from the might of the field mice and more from the mysterious forces of swapping. With the terrific sniffing of their glistening, blackcurrant noses, the moles were best at collecting the pungent fungi which grew deep underground in the Bottom Corner. The moles' favourite thing to eat, the other creatures thought them an acquired taste, preferring the shimmering stones, like little frozen water droplets, also only found in the Bottom Corner. With noses far better at smelling than their beady eyes were at seeing, the moles were not very good at finding the stones. They had no smell and, with no sunlight underground, catching their glimmer in the deep darkness was impossible. Still, the upstanding fellows that they were, the moles had agreements with other creatures they had to honour. More importantly, though, the moles had become partial to the delicious foods from other areas and could not bear the thought of living without them. Rather than sniffing out the fungi like they had used to, the moles spent more of their days digging longer and wider tunnels, hoping that they would simply bump into the stones, hearing them clack on their digging claws. As their most favourite food, with less fungi collected, many moles often had little to eat. Trying to solve this problem, many families made their young moles start hunting for precious stones as soon as their digging claws were long enough. Before the moles started swapping things, this would have been unheard of; being a pup was when a mole had fun and learnt how to be happy and polite!

Often many days passed between a sparkling stone being found, which was hard for the moles. With far less fungi than before and few stones to swap for food, they got hungrier and hungrier. When a long while passed without finding any stones, as was becoming more common, the flow of things to the Bottom Corner from other areas slowed to a trickle. 'If these moles are having nothing to be giving us, we should be giving them our fruits, why?' the shrews complained loudly as they sat looking at big piles of berries and crab apples they could not eat themselves rotting in the early summer sun.

'They want more dried fish?' the otters cried in despair. 'They can have fish when we have more of those shiny stones!'

Being determined creatures, the moles dug deeper, wider tunnels. They had to find more stones; their empty tummies relied upon it. And dig they did. Before long, the Bottom Corner looked like the moon hovering on a clear summer's evening, suspended like a plump white peach from a tree, its pock-marked surface so foreign from the Field's lush grass. How quickly things could change. The Bottom Corner became pitted as many tunnels collapsed, yet the moles continued to dig in vain, hoping they would strike luck.

They got hungrier still; there was no luck to strike. The food arriving from the other creatures stopped altogether.

12

S imilar things were happening in other areas of the Field too. Many creatures, taken with the splendour of the Hedgerow, began swapping what they had for more precious stones and golden nuggets rather than important things like food and wood. With access to many interesting and useful things from all over the Field, the need for some went up as more creatures wanted them, like the fish and shrimp caught by the otters. Until now, only the otters had relied on them, catching just the right amount, which they had been doing far longer than they could remember. But the otters wanted silky cloth, shiny stones, wood and fruits like all the other creatures, and they only had dried fish and shrimp to swap for these. With more creatures than the otters eating what the River provided, there was not enough to go around.

Many other creatures also started noticing things in the Field were not the same as they used to be; things were changing. The number of silky pods the grey squirrels collected was getting fewer and fewer as well. Starting small, so neither the field mice nor grey squirrels really noticed or were worried by it, as the seasons passed, the difference in the amount collected now and the season before got greater. The Queen and her advisors spent many long evenings debating why it could be, to no avail. They kept it secret, but the grey squirrels had noticed too, and they knew why. Every silky pod had a little worm inside and every pod collected was one less worm that would grow into a butterfly that laid lots of eggs that hatched into worms that wove more silky pods. For every pod the field mice forced the grey squirrels to collect, there were fewer for the next season, and the season after that.

Living in their new palaces removed from everyday life in the Copse, enjoying the success of the field mice, it took the rajahs a long while to notice what was happening. It was not until the Governor Prince began visiting the rajahs and getting angry with each of them in turn that they realised. But it was no good. The rajahs had never seen this happen; they did not know what to do. The field mice continued to wash, stamp, spin, weave and swap silky cloth at a rapid pace. There were many things they needed to swap it for. They thought the huge stores of silky pods they had built up in the Warren would never run out. They were wrong. The new looms wove silky cloth far quicker than before, emptying the stores in a blink. Before long, many looms in the Hedgerow were standing still with no pods left to weave. It was too late. Never again would these looms weave the beautiful, shimmery cloth that had quickly become the pride of the field mice.

When this happened, things started to change in the Copse. Caught up negotiating the swapping of their silky cloth with all the other creatures in the Field, the Queen had given the rajahs more freedom to look after their bit of the Copse, relieving her of this burden. But, as far as she was concerned, this had not worked. Every season there were fewer silky pods collected and she thought that this was the rajahs' fault. As the flow of silky pods from the Copse slowed, the Queen sent more soldiers from the Hedgerow to force the grey squirrels to spend longer collecting them and to make sure none went missing. It barely made a difference. After the sun had blown a kiss goodbye to the horizon, many grey squirrels still went home to their hollows after a long day scouring the top branches of the mulberry trees without having found a single silky pod.

The Governor Prince passed this news back to the Queen and she became worried, immediately calling a special meeting with her advisors. For some seasons now, although there had been lots of silky pods, the Queen had felt the Copse was becoming a drain on the Hedgerow, requiring more soldiers and food to be sent, which they now had little of themselves. Since the field mice had stopped the grey squirrels foraging for food so they could collect more silky pods, the Copse relied completely on food from the Hedgerow, which itself relied upon other areas. With almost no pods to turn into cloth, the stores of cloth in the Warren, built up as more was weaved than the field mice could swap, got smaller too. Soon there was hardly enough cloth for the field mice to make snug jackets for themselves, let alone to swap. When this happened, the Queen made a difficult decision: the Hedgerow was to go back to swapping wood, just like it had originally done with the otters all those seasons ago. Unfortunately for the field mice, this did not work either. Many areas already had lots of wood and were collecting and trying to swap it too. With so much wood in the Field, and much of it stronger and easier to carve than the Hedgerow's, most creatures were unwilling to swap anything very interesting for what the field mice had to offer.

With their unusual flat, colourful hats and strange, tongue-clicking language, the ferrets from the Thicket were good at sneaking into the Copse when the grey squirrels and field mice soldiers were asleep, gathering wood that fell from the oak trees. Sneakily tip-toeing from the Copse laden with their bundles, the ferrets swapped it with other areas, getting far more in return than the field mice could get for their flimsy Hedgerow wood. This worked well for many creatures. The otter elders, realising the dwindling number of fish and shrimp in the River was because far more were being caught than before, decided to swap less of them. With the ferrets' cunning tricks, the otters still got the same amount of wood as they had from the field mice before.

Just like the moles before them, who had run out of things to swap, the grey squirrels started to go hungry too. Weaving less cloth and not swapping much wood, the field mice had little food for themselves, so they gave even less to the Copse. The rajahs, realising the pickle the field mice were in, used it to their advantage. Slyly, they kept the same amount of food as before for themselves, using what was left to encourage the hungrier grey squirrels to do things for them. In doing so, they made their armies bigger and had even more lavish palaces carved in the oldest oak tree trunks.

The rajahs were happy; they did not want anything to change. While bad for the field mice and the rest of the grey squirrels, this situation was good for them; they were more important than ever before. But this came at a cost. Outside the comfort of their palaces, the rajahs did not realise the other creatures in the Copse were very, very unhappy.

13

The resistance to the field mice started out among the grey squirrels like a small virus at the end of one autumn. After a string of long, cold winters with little food, the grey squirrels nervously looked at the prospect of yet another the same. One oppressive grey morning, as the winter was settling in, some grey squirrels blankly refused to collect silky pods when soldiers from a rajah's army ordered them to do so. The rebellion quickly grew, spreading from the simple refusal to collect silky pods to the ruining of the few already collected, waiting in piles at the edge of the Copse to be lugged across the Field to the Hedgerow. To solve matters, the rajahs did what they thought the field mice would, telling their soldiers to use spear butts and the flat of their swords' blades to beat those responsible for causing the fuss. At its worst, the favourite punishment of the old grey squirrel Chief was used, the ringleaders tied upside down by their tails at the top of the tallest oak in that rajah's part of the Copse for a whole moon cycle.

Unfortunately, this did not deliver any more food for the hungry creatures in the Copse and things worsened. Frost after frost followed one another like a procession of grey squirrels lugging silky pods across the Field. The soldiers in the rajahs' armies, although a little better off than most grey squirrels, started to go hungry as well, the Queen sending less food as she tried starving the rebels into behaving themselves. The soldiers got hungrier and began to lose faith in the rajahs, seeing them for what they really were: puppets of the field mice. Unhappy doing what the rajahs wanted them to, the beatings the soldiers were ordered to give the rebels almost stopped.

When the first signs of the uprising had emerged, the rajahs had secretly met in a thick bramble bush in a remote part of the Copse, as far away from the Hedgerow and Governor Prince as possible. Here they agreed that the Queen could not find out about the uprisings. Her response if she learnt the rajahs were not doing as she wanted them did not bear thinking about. As much as the rajahs tried, the Queen had creatures hidden all over the Field, feeding titbits of information back to the Hedgerow, and it was not long before she knew that something was up. She was unhappy the Governor Prince had not realised first…

Calling a meeting with her advisors, the Queen told them what she was going to do rather than asking for their advice. After the meeting, she ordered a hundred score more soldiers from the Hedgerow's army to leave immediately for the Copse, instructing them to use their weapons to bring the rebels back into line. She did not realise it, but this was more of the same for the grey squirrels. It did not solve their problems and did little to change what they were doing, making them angrier and more rebellious still.

After the violent beating of a gang of grey squirrel luggers by a score of field mice soldiers, the frustration boiled over. Dragging a sled with some of the very last silky pods from the Copse across the Field's dewy grass, some luggers stopped suddenly and, using nothing but their teeth and claws, set upon the soldiers, inflicting dreadful wounds before fleeing. News of the upset travelled quickly around the Field, embarrassing the Queen greatly. She despised the thought that any creature in the Field felt anything but fear and envy towards the Hedgerow, and this escape made it look weak and unorganised. To prove the Hedgerow was as strong as ever, the displeased Queen decided to punish the grey squirrels. Searching in soaking rain, glorious sunshine, and everything in between, a hundred score field mice soldiers linked forepaws and marched across the Field in search of the reckless band of luggers. Where the Riverbank met the Backwater, the gang were found, cowering by the water's edge, not too scared to face the River's chilly wetness, but too scared to face the unknown on the other side.

To make an example of the troublesome escapees, the Queen chose a favourite old punishment of the field mice: a beating with spear shafts – but with one big difference. Where this would usually be done somewhere only the soldiers doing the beating could see, the Queen ordered that all creatures in the Copse be forced to watch. It had the desired effect, the grey squirrels lining the branches of the oak trees around the Copse's biggest clearing looked down at the beating below, shaking with fear. While the Queen thought the beating would do little more than scare the grey squirrels into behaving again, it humiliated the rajahs, who felt it reflected their inability to control the rebels. Finally, having had enough of being ordered about by the Queen, half the rajahs, acting separately from one another, turned against the field mice.

Many grey squirrels who spent their days trying to collect silky pods or lugging them to the Hedgerow stopped these things and joined the fighting against the field mice, but not in the rajahs' armies. Rather, they formed their own rebel groups instead. Fighting engulfed the Copse once more, the rajahs' armies not only attacking the Hedgerow's soldiers, but those of other rajahs and the rebels who fought for them too. Defeating soldiers from another part of the Copse, the rajahs absorbed them into their own armies before continuing.

This happened in all but one corner of the Copse where the trees grew closer together and the brambles crawled around and between trunks forming a thick barrier, making it easily defendable by the rajah who ruled there. Knowing his unique advantage, this rajah refused to side with the field mice or any other rajahs. Instead, he claimed his part of the Copse as neutral in all the goings-on of the other creatures of the Copse and Field, making the decision in the best interests of the grey squirrels he ruled. Rarely used and oft-forgotten, an ancient agreement between all the Field's creatures made sure this rajah's decision was respected. With the most defensible part of the Copse now off-limits and its army no longer needing to fight, gaining independence from the field mice became even more difficult for the grey squirrels.

14

The Queen's power in the Copse dwindled whenever one rajah defeated another and their armies combined, making the armies of the successful rajahs bigger and stronger. In response to this, she had few options other than to continue sending more brave field mouse soldiers across the Field to join the fighting. Barely understanding why it was happening or who was fighting who, these soldiers were a long way from home. It made no sense to them, but they loved the Hedgerow and they loved their Queen; if she wanted them to do something, of course they would do it, and she knew this.

Angry grey squirrels were not the Queen's only problem. The small groups of rebellious rabbits which had met secretly for many seasons in the Warren's hidden tunnels caught wind of the problems in the Copse. Although not renowned as the cunningest of creatures, the rabbits were patient, watching many field mice soldiers leave the Hedgerow, few returning home again. With a mere few dozen score soldiers left defending the Hedgerow, the rabbit rebels saw the opportunity they had been waiting many long seasons for. From behind paws as they rummaged for berries and nuts and collected wood, word travelled that various small rebellious groups had joined together, their secret leaders deciding to follow the grey squirrels' example and pursue their own long, lost freedom. The Queen's spies listened intently to all goings-on in the Hedgerow and it was not long before she sensed the rabbits were up to something and quickly ordered most of the field mouse soldiers back from the Copse. The tides turned, now only a few dozen score soldiers were left in the Copse trying to regain order of the unruly rajahs and the countless angry grey squirrels now fighting for them.

When the last score of field mice soldiers summoned back to the Hedgerow were leaving the Copse, the grey squirrels, now mostly united under one rajah, gave chase and there was a brutal, bloody slaughter. Upon killing the last field mouse soldier himself, this rajah stood in front of his army and the rebels supporting him. He wiped the blood from his wooden dagger with an ancient silky cloth woven long ago. Folding the cloth, he tucked it neatly inside his shimmery jacket woven in the Hedgerow. To loud cheering, he announced that the Copse now belonged to all the grey squirrels, not the Chief or the field mouse Queen, and that he was to be leader until another was chosen. For the first while in many whiles, something resembling happiness crept into the Copse. The grey squirrels joyfully swung from oak tree to oak tree singing raucously of the blissful freedom that lay ahead of them. Little did they know, the joy was to be all too brief.

At a similar moment, just as the last of the field mice soldiers arrived back in the Hedgerow from the Copse, the rebellious rabbits met in a far-flung corner of the Warren. Sitting in a circle, they blew dust off a plan scrawled in mulberry juice ink on a thick cloth woven from the malting winter coats of rabbits many seasons before. Hidden at the end of the darkest, dankest tunnel in the Warren since the earliest days of the field mouse invasion, the rebels voted to put the plan into action with no changes (for it was very thorough and sensible). The plan outlined that, when the moment was right, every rabbit would flee the Hedgerow and run underground into the Warren, digging ferociously to cover all the entrances. Once barricaded in, the plan judged that the Hedgerow's emergency food supplies stored in the Warren, although quite stale and mouldy, would keep the rabbits going while they waited patiently for the field mice to lose interest in trying to get them out. Finally, the plan described how the secret leader of the rebels would come forward from the shadows of mystery and take control of the Warren until the old rabbit Tsar or one of his family could return from exile with the hares in the Divet to rule once more.

15

Despite the lead rajah's best intentions, the grey squirrels were struggling to find a new leader for the Copse. Even after all the fighting he had done to bring the Copse together, the Rajah did not think he should become leader automatically, believing the grey squirrels should choose who led them. In the Field, a strong creature with a big army usually always became leader, doing what they could to make sure their position could never be taken away from them or their family. While noble, the Rajah's idea was an unusual one. Although the Chief and Queen were now gone, the defeated rajahs were still there, leading supporters who were unhappy that the lead rajah of the Copse was not their rajah. As well as this, each defeated rajah still entertained the thought they might become ruler of the Copse and were unwilling to support any other creature but themselves. The grey squirrels faced a problem.

The different bits of the Copse given to the rajahs had not existed before the field mice invasion. Rather, the Queen had just divided the Copse willy-nilly to keep the grey squirrels in check and make it easier to collect silky pods and give food to those who could no longer collect their own. When this worked well, the Governor Prince did the same thing again, dividing all the parts of the Copse into even smaller bits which he then gave to even more rajahs. Although neither the Queen, Governor Prince, nor any of the Queen's advisors, had thought of it, over the seasons, grey squirrels became very proud of the bit of the Copse they lived in. This passion fuelled a rivalry between the creatures of the different bits to collect the most silky pods, carve the biggest hollow for their rajah and get the most food from the Hedgerow. Such was this pride, any thought of joining with grey squirrels from another part to rebel against the field mice was unimaginable. This meant that, for quite a while, the rajahs posed little threat to the Queen's rule.

During the fighting, although different parts of the Copse gradually combined as rajahs with stronger armies beat those with weaker armies, each grey squirrel's love for their bit remained strong. Now the moment had come to choose a new leader, who it was agreed would be known as the Premier, the grey squirrels were divided. Some from smaller parts realised it unlikely that their rajah, who had been easily defeated by the other rajahs, would ever become leader. Not wanting their bit to be ruled by a rajah from another bit, they chose to start fighting again, now for their bit's independence from the Copse entirely. On the other paw, larger bits with stronger fighters and more confidence in their rajah to become Premier, started fighting again to try and make it happen and prevent smaller parts from breaking free – they wanted their rajah to rule as much of the Copse as possible. Either way, the grey squirrels once again felt that they only had one choice: they had to fight. It was the only way to make sure they had a leader who would make things happier for them, their children and their children's children in the seasons to come.

This new round of fighting in the Copse was some of the most complicated ever seen in the Field. Parts fighting to be separate fought parts wishing for the Copse to remain united. Grey squirrels wanting their rajah to become Premier fought against those from parts who wanted to be separate and also those wanting their rajah to be Premier. And in some parts, where no creature could decide what they wanted, they simply fought amongst themselves. What a mess!

Seasons passed and the bloody fighting continued. Sometimes, in the summer, when the sun's rays penetrated the thick oak canopy, baking the earth around the base of the trees as hard as Riverbank stone, the battle eased and the fighters rested in the shade. Sometimes, in the winter, when the icy wind whistled through the Copse, bare oak branches doing little to soften its bite, the fighting stopped altogether, although only briefly; it was too cold for paws to hold swords. Otherwise, the fighting went on and on.

Strange as it may seem, peace was still at the fore of the grey squirrel's minds, they just did not want any old peace. The rajahs made many attempts to stop the fighting for a moon or two – just long enough for them to meet and discuss stopping the fighting altogether. Often special agreements to do this were drafted, but they never got pawprints from all rajahs pressed upon them side by side.

Why? Happiness for one part always cost the happiness of another. Some rajahs would like the agreement and add their pawprint, others did not, refusing to add theirs.

Over the seasons, grey squirrels, irrespective of which part of the Copse they were from, grew unhappy with their rajah who had failed to lead them to a promised victory and end the fighting. Slowly but surely, these unhappy creatures' anger turned away from the grey squirrels from other bits of the Copse who looked the same, spoke the same and wanted much the same things as they did, to the rajahs themselves. Still intoxicated by the power the Queen had given them many moons before, although she no longer had anything to do with the Copse, the rajahs did not see it coming. Just like the Queen, each rajah believed that they had been chosen by something, somewhere to lead the Copse to peace and happiness. Now, the fighting changed once more, the grey squirrels turning upon their rajahs, overthrowing them in quick, bloody battles which often left the rajah dead and the creature who killed them the new leader.

Yet, as parts of the Copse were overcome and merged with others, rule transferring to a new leader, much as had happened when they were fighting to be free from the field mice, each grey squirrel's love for their bit of the Copse stayed strong. Driven out as those who defeated them moved in, the expelled creatures were forced to wander the Copse looking for another part where they could live safely and peacefully – something they rarely found.

Wherever they roamed in the Copse, the creatures living in the bits where the wanderers arrived thought them untrustworthy and different, although they were mostly the

16

The wanderers quickly tired of being unable to find somewhere in the Copse to settle and belong again. Shuffling wearily from one part of the Copse to another, carrying their kittens on their backs, they huddled together uncomfortably wherever they found some shelter. Before falling asleep after a long day wandering, they prayed that they would wake up somewhere in the morning far away from the fighting; somewhere where they would be safe, have food and belong. When they awoke to the sun forcing its shimmering fingers through the thick oak canopy above and realised that their wishes had not come true, their hearts sank in their furry chests. They felt like they were clinging frantically to a log floating down the churning River after heavy rains, tossed here and there, having no say where they were going or what would happen. They only wanted to get to safety.

The wanderers felt lonely: like the god they believed in was not there with them and they had to do everything themselves. Realising this, they knew the only thing that would change their luck was if they grasped it in their own paws and made it themselves. So, they did. If things were not going to change in the Copse, they needed to look outside of it.

Starting in small numbers which grew and grew, the wanderers left the Copse to explore the Field, searching for somewhere they could fit in and call home. Drifting from area to area, from the Riverbank to the Watermeadow, the Backwater to the Thicket; they were often welcomed with open forepaws. When the first few wanderers arrived in an area, the creatures who called it home thought it exciting to have different creatures living with them. But, as the seasons rolled on and more wanderers arrived, this welcome often changed as the original creatures began to worry that there was no longer enough space or food. As seasons passed, this worry grew, the leaders of many areas introducing limits on the number of wanderers they allowed to live with them.

Leaders did this for different reasons. The otter elders knew there was little space for new burrows on the Riverbank and a limited number of fish and shrimp in the River. For the badger Lord, it was simply that grey squirrels could not see well underground and got lost in the dark maze of tunnels in the Sett. Aside from these reasons, and many others like them, the wanderers, whichever creatures they joined and no matter how welcoming they were, always found it hard to fit in. Those who joined the otters had never eaten fish or shrimp before, preferring acorns, which was what they had always eaten until the field mice came along. They had also never lived in burrows or close by water, finding the trickling noises and dampness unsettling. It did not feel like home; they liked being high above the ground, the breeze ruffling their coats and tickling their whiskers. These were things that made the grey squirrels different and meant they never felt the same as the other creatures they lived with. To whichever area the wanderers moved, they often lived together, carving hollows or building drays next to one another, using what they could to make things a little more like the Copse: the home they were forced to leave.

Sticking together and separating themselves from the other creatures in their new homes only made things worse. As the wanderers became more isolated, the other creatures looked upon the wanderers as outcasts, making rude jokes about them and their differences: the shape of their ears, their language, which sounded like the noise came from their noses, and the different colour of their shimmering fur and silky jackets they wore. For those living with the practical otters, the jokes mostly concerned the wanderers' inability to swim and catch fish and shrimp. But neither could they dig burrows very well or master Otter, with its many sounds that emerged mysteriously from the back of the throat. The wanderers kept their furry chins up and consoled themselves by trying to make part of the Riverbank more like the Copse by planting acorns to grow oak trees. If they could not go home, maybe a bit of their home could come to them. Unfortunately, oak trees take a long while to grow and are not fond of having a brimming river as a neighbour. The wanderers' plan failed dismally. Still, the jolly creatures that they were, wherever they were living and whoever they were living with, the wanderers always managed to look on the bright side. It was better than being in the Copse, where the fighting kept on and on and peace was no closer than the day they had wandered away.

Few grey squirrels regretted leaving the Copse, although they missed it very much; the tall oak trees with their strong limbs to skip across, the dappled sunlight filtering through the emerald kaleidoscope canopy above and the comforting smell of gently decaying leaves. When new wanderers shuffled exhaustedly into different areas seeking peace and safety, they always told the same story to their new neighbours: the ground beneath the oaks in the Copse was becoming uneven with the graves of those killed in the fighting. In the early spring, daffodils and snowdrops sprouted around the edges of the graves in the fresh earth, the only beautiful thing to be seen in the Copse for many seasons. It seemed as if an endless winter of unhappiness had descended when the field mice invaded all those seasons before, and it had clung to oak trunks, hidden in hollows and buried itself in the leaf litter ever since.

17

In the Hedgerow, things had taken another turn for the worse for the Queen. The rats, seeing the rabbit's success regaining their freedom, made the most of the chaos as the field mice soldiers tried to regain control of the rabbits and the Warren. The rats' wish to be free was different from the grey squirrels and rabbits. They no longer had an area of the Field to call home, a place to go if and when they escaped. Complicating matters, the rats had lived under field mice rule for so long that they had forgotten how to fight and did not have the secret rebel groups and special plan the rabbits had. So, they had to do things differently. Instead of picking up swords and spears like every other creature in the Field had done when faced with a problem like theirs, the rats simply stopped rummaging for food, collecting wood and carving things. They stopped doing anything for the field mice entirely.

The Queen was not expecting this new disruption to life in the Hedgerow. Having not learnt her lesson, she dealt with the rats the same way she had the grey squirrels. When the rats refused to do anything, lazing about on their backs in the dappled sunlight filtered by the Hedgerow's upper branches, the Queen ordered her soldiers to use their swords and spears to force the rats back to rummaging, collecting and carving. But the smell of freedom had filled their nostrils and gone too deep into their lungs. No matter how much the field mouse soldiers slashed and stabbed, the rats refused to return to doing the things the Queen wanted them to.

Most field mice were unable to wander around their Hedgerow without seeing a rat being threatened or beaten by soldiers. This made them angry and they channelled this fury back towards the Queen; it was up to her to keep the Hedgerow safe and make sure they all had food and wood to build nests. She was not doing this and neither they nor the rats were safe and happy. These brutal tactics, which had ultimately failed in the Copse, did so too in the Hedgerow. But most field mice had known little of what was happening to the grey squirrels, having not been in the Copse seeing what the field mouse soldiers were doing with their own eyes. Being so far away, stories of the goings-on in the Copse barely made their way back to the Hedgerow, so the field mice had been ignorant with no need to be unhappy.

Now it was happening in the Hedgerow. Besides having little food or wood because the rats were no longer collecting it, the field mice grew angry at how the rats were being treated. They were their fellow creatures; they breathed, had families, and felt happiness and sadness just like them. As the Queen ordered her soldiers to become even stricter, many field mice pushed aside their prejudices of how lowly they thought the rats. They formed small groups and met secretly in the early evenings as the stars did the same above, to debate at length what was happening in the Hedgerow and what could be done to fix it. In the end, all conversations came back to the Queen and what she was doing to solve the problem. Realising lots of little groups were powerless against the Hedgerow's army, one summer's day, the field mice agreed to join together to form one big group outside the Queen's palace. Chanting and singing, they were all in favour of stopping the army's attacks against the rats, letting them be free to live in the Hedgerow as they pleased, equals to the field mice.

Beyond this wish, the group paid little regard to practical matters. Who would gather food and wood? When one of the ringleaders asked this question from a branch to the seething crowd below, the response was silence. No field mouse, however old and wise or young and clever, had an answer. At that moment, the anger of the field mice intensified. Having originally stemmed from unhappiness at the rats' mistreatment, the groups' anger morphed into something new, as they realised how unhappy they were with the Queen and how she was looking after their home. They no longer had any silky pods to weave into their favourite cloth. This had become their great pride and it upset them greatly. The lack of food was another thing. They were reliant upon the other creatures in the Field for it but had few things they could swap now their stores of silky cloth had run out. The number of soldiers sent to the Copse was one thing more. This had split families, often for many seasons. Maybe the rabbits would not have rebelled if there had been more soldiers to keep them in line? All these things, they decided, may not have happened if they, the ordinary field mice, were making the decisions, not just the Queen and her advisors.

The Queen was caught. Unable to get the rats to do the things she needed them to, and now facing an uprising from her very own creatures, she did something drastic to protect herself and the Hedgerow. After a rushed discussion with her advisors, she announced that the rats would have their freedom and gave them a small piece of the Hedgerow to call their own and rule as they pleased. Like most things the Queen did, there was a catch. She attached a single condition to their freedom. When the rats chose a new leader, they would have to add their pawprint to an agreement outlining how the two parts of the Hedgerow acted towards one another and the Field's other areas. Most importantly, this agreement would make sure anything each side wanted to swap was offered to the other before other areas.

Beyond this, the Queen offered the rats no help working out how they should organise themselves and make decisions, or what they could swap with who, what type of leader they should have and how they would be chosen. Although free from the field mice, the rats' situation descended into turmoil almost immediately.

Having spent so long under the strict rule of the field mice, the rats were now scared of not being free, each of them doing all they could to make sure no other rat had too much control over anything. To help with this, rats wanting similar things formed groups to make decisions about particular aspects of daily life in their new part of the Hedgerow. With strong opinions about what the rats should now do, these groups tried to control how decisions were made, meeting to choose everything from which berries to pick and wood to collect, to which field mouse words should be included in the rat language. (The rats thought using words from Field Mouse was far more sophisticated than just using Rat.)

Each of these groups were open for any rat to join, as long as they felt the same way about what the group wanted as the other members. New groups were constantly formed and the number of members in each grew quickly as more rats wanted to become involved in making decisions. With more creatures in each group sharing their different views, things became chaotic and it was soon decided each group needed a leader to run meetings and make sure the right decisions were being made. So, every now and again, each group got together and voted to choose one. While this improved things a little, not long after this, most of the rats agreed it would be better to just have one group making decisions rather than lots of smaller ones, as many groups making decisions on lots of little things was very complicated and wasted much effort. But which group would be this group? Obviously each one and its leader wanted to be, but, because there could only be one, it was finally agreed that every few seasons all the rats would come together and have another vote to choose which group and leader they wanted to make all the decisions until the next vote came around.

As brilliant as it sounded, with no experience leading, voting or even organising how to run daily life and make decisions, as they had never needed to under the field mice, the rats struggled to make the plan happen. This meant decisions were not made about important things, like forming an army or making rules to decide how rats should act towards one another, protecting them and the things that belonged to them, much as other areas had. None of the leaders of these new groups could even agree on what being a rat was or the things that rats should do and say and want.

In the midst of this chaos, rats from some groups gathered together small bands of followers. Offering extra food or the promise of an important position when they became leader of the rats, a bit like the rajahs had done, these new rogue leaders did the opposite of what the rats had done against the field mice. Using skills perfected during their days under the field mice, the leaders encouraged their followers to carve swords and spears and use them to threaten other rats to vote for them or prevent other leaders from opposing them. The strength of each of the few leaders doing this grew and weakened in an endless wave, their followers continually changing their minds and supporting another leader who promised them more food or a more important position. Leader after leader was voted in and then removed, each failing miserably to do what really needed to be done: ensuring peace and providing food and shelter for all.

Yet this only scratched the surface of the problems compounded by so long spent being controlled by the field mice. Aside from carving swords and spears to threaten one another, many of the other things the rats had become good at doing under the field mice were now no longer useful. The Field's other creatures now mostly chose to collect their own wood and carve their own swords and spears. Having spent so long doing this, the rats had forgotten most of the things they had known about before, like how to weave grasses, and about which grew where, and which were the best for making different things like baskets, nests and hats. Unsure of what they should be doing and unable to organise themselves or agree on a leader who could decide how to do it, the rats could not unite in a way to do anything which led to any meaningful swapping with the Field's other creatures.

18

I n the other half of the Hedgerow, the Queen, to save her and her family's rule, decided to meet her angry subjects halfway in their request for more of a say in how decisions were made. She ordered another smaller palace be built not far from her own where a group of representatives would meet to make decisions. Voted by all field mice to represent them and their views every third autumn on the day the first hawthorn leaf turned red, the two score field mice with the most votes became the representatives who then had a vote among themselves to choose a leader known as the Prime Minister. The representatives then spent the next three seasons discussing how they thought the Hedgerow should be run. When a decision on something was made, like how much food each soldier in the army should be given or what should be swapped with who and when, it was scrawled in curly shapes on a dried chestnut leaf and taken to the Queen. Studying it carefully, she then ruled whether the representatives' decision was a good one, placing her pawprint in mulberry juice ink at the bottom if she thought that it was.

The Queen was very proud of this new way of doing things. She still ruled the Hedgerow but passed on the difficult decision making, which had become far more complex in recent seasons with the swapping and fighting, to the representatives. Shaken by the uprising against her, and fearful that it might happen again, the Queen now whiled away her days doing things which made the field mice feel good. Things like opening new nests, visiting the sick, and watching the army parade backwards and forwards in front of her palace showing off their shiny jackets and the elaborate carving of their swords and spears. Still as important as before, this change in doing things protected the Queen against further uprisings; the representatives made the decisions and they were chosen. There was little need for any field mouse to get angry with her now.

In return for listening to them and giving them a say in how decisions were made, the opinions of most field mice about the Queen went back to how they used to be: she was wise and good and they were all very proud of having her as their queen. Still, there were some who thought the changes were not a good idea. They felt that the fact the Hedgerow had lost things they had always thought important, like loyalty and respect for the Queen and having other creatures to do things for them they did not want to do, was sad. They were unable to see why ordinary field mice needed to choose representatives and be involved in making decisions. It was a burden they were unwilling to bear.

Like the grey squirrel wanderers who felt they no longer belonged in the Copse, these field mice chose to do the same thing, leaving the Hedgerow to find new homes in other areas of the Field. An identical thing happened in the other half of the Hedgerow as well. Many rats, frustrated by the continuous changing of leader and lack of decisions to make sure they had something to eat and somewhere to live, went wandering too.

Lots of rabbits in the Warren felt the same way and joined. Like the rats, they had found returning to freedom and the Warren difficult. Haunted by memories of the illness all those seasons before, many of them realised being free did not mean things were better. Making matters worse, after returning to the Warren, the rabbits discovered that their Tsar, whose family had been living with the hares, had recently died. Following rabbit tradition, his son, the Tsarevich, took charge. Born and raised alongside young hares in the Divet, before his return to the Warren the new Tsar had never met a rabbit other than his mother, father, brothers and sisters. Never thinking that they would go back to the Warren and he would become Tsar, when he was growing up, little had been done to prepare him for the responsibility. The new Tsar knew nothing of what the rabbits had done in the past or what made them special; he could barely even speak Rabbit.

2

THE RISE

19

The grey squirrels, field mice, rats and rabbits, unhappy with their lives where their families had always called home, wished for food, shelter and safety, unchained from things that had happened in the past. To make these wishes come true, they wanted the opportunity to do what they pleased. If they put effort into collecting or making something, they wanted it to be good for them, not for a queen, rajah or tsar who ruled them.

Such a place for a new beginning did exist, safe from the turmoil of their old homes. In a far-flung corner of the Field few creatures ever visited was the Rise, home to the weasels. Keeping mostly to themselves, like the badgers, there had been a short and bloody fight among the weasels many seasons previously. So horrible was the fighting, things in the Rise had been turned upside down, everything that had happened before destroyed, allowing the weasels to start anew. Thanks to the tireless commitment of many generations, the Rise had become quite different to the Field's other areas: a place no creature ordered another about, where all were free, treated the same and could have their own things without fear of them being taken away. If a creature collected lots of food or wood, they could keep it instead of having it taken to be used or swapped by a queen or chief. Leading and making all the decisions was the President, who was voted in every few seasons by all the creatures who called the Rise home.

While things in the Rise seemed to work quite well, it had not always been this way. After the horrible fighting many seasons before, half a dozen weasels had met and discussed their vision of the wonderful place the Rise should become. But, when they tried to realise their dream, they had had no luck; the Rise was simply too big and there were not enough weasels to fill it. The fighting had killed many weasels and destroyed most of the nests in the middle of the Rise where they lived, leaving nothing but piles of sticks, mud and carcasses. To escape the destruction, many weasels moved away to far-flung corners of the Rise where creatures had never lived before. With great distances between them, it was hard for the weasels to swap things among themselves, let alone with the other creatures in the Field. So, unlike most other areas, life for the weasels did not change to revolve around the constant need to swap more things and the Rise had not become reliant upon other areas for things like food, as the field mice had. For these reasons, there were far fewer creatures living there than other areas, and those that did had not changed to focus only on collecting and making things they had a lot of, were good at or creatures in other areas wanted more of.

With so much space and so few weasels, there was lots of

room in the Rise for many more creatures – there were many bits the weasels had still not even been to. Treating every creature the same, no matter who they were or where they were from, meant the weasels welcomed wandering creatures looking for new lives with open forepaws. Whether from the Hedgerow, Warren or Copse, all were welcome to join the weasels' dream of making a place where every creature could do what they wanted, how they wanted, with who they wanted.

Stories of the Rise and its wonderful freedom spread around the Field and many creatures made the long journey there. Settling in quickly, with lots of food, space and wood to make nests from, these new arrivals immediately adopted the unique understanding that existed among all creatures who called the Rise home: that every one of them, while special and good at different things, wanted the same thing and should be treated the same. As more creatures moved there, a new language began to emerge too, combining words from different languages spoken by creatures all over the Field. Both these things, and much determination from the newly settled wanderers who wanted to make the most of their new lives, helped the Rise to start making and collecting many things very effectively indeed.

The system of swapping in the Field had gradually become more complicated and many creatures, like the grey squirrels and moles, lost out, unable to be involved very well. The knowledge and skills of the newly arrived creatures provided a great opportunity for the Rise, which usually did things slightly differently than the other areas. For starters, the Rise began swapping things it could turn into other things and swap again for more of the same or something else. They swapped large chestnuts and blossom nectar for the straightest wood from the Copse and then, using skills learnt from the rats and rabbits who now called the Rise home, carved this wood into swords and spears which they swapped back to the grey squirrels, as well as to the field mice and otters for other useful things. The variety of skills brought by the wanderers meant the Rise was able to choose to collect or make things some areas wanted more and were willing to swap the most for. Soon, the Rise was just as good at swapping as the Hedgerow had been, but it had not taken nearly as long. As word spread of the wonderous things happening in the Rise, more and more creatures packed up their lives and made the long journey across the Field to live there. Even creatures from areas like the Watermeadow and Riverbank, without the problems of the Copse or Warren, wanted to try life in the Rise for themselves; every creature in the Field was talking about it.

Choosing a leader for the Rise was far easier than the grey squirrels and rats had found. All its creatures generally wanted the same thing and there were few disagreements, so the President was chosen much like other areas had started doing, by having a vote. In seasons past, the dozen weasels had given much thought to their vision for the Rise. They thought that the President should only be voted in for a few seasons so they could not change things to benefit themselves or their friends. Seeing that this worked well, creatures from many other areas started looking up to the Rise for guidance. Realising the Rise's influence was growing, the President had an interesting thought: if other areas became more like the

Rise, maybe the creatures in these areas might become as free and happy as they were.

A grey squirrel who had himself only fled the Copse a few seasons before, the President also wondered that, if other areas of the Field became more like the Rise, perhaps it might be good for the Rise too. One warm summer evening, unable to sleep, the President sat on a moon-silver branch in the top of the cedar tree which held his palace, looking out over the Field below him. With the stars winking playfully above, he wondered if there would be more swapping in the Field if other areas did what the Rise had done, attracting many creatures from other areas who knew how to do lots of different things. To the President, swapping was happiness, but not swapping in the way it was usually done. Having more food to eat and warm things to wear was certainly good for all creatures but, up until now, swapping had also had its downsides. With many areas more reliant upon others than ever before, some creatures got stuck collecting or making things they were not good at, like the moles and their shiny stones. Even worse, this reliance meant unrest could spread quickly from one area to another, like it had from the Copse to the Hedgerow.

Many creatures in the Rise had left their homes because of these problems and they now felt it was their duty to bring to other areas the peace and opportunities they were lucky to have themselves. Gathering his most trusted friends and advisors, the President came up with a plan to use swapping to help the areas of the Field having the most trouble.

20

While a wonderful thought, just before the President was able to put his plan into action, fighting broke out in the Field once more. As had become the case so often in recent seasons, swapping was of course to blame, the fighting now being over who, given their recent troubles, would replace the field mice as the creatures who controlled it. To most creatures, this new round of fighting, started by the shrews from the Backwater, came as a surprise. The shrews were usually peaceful creatures. This had changed and the shrews were envious of the Hedgerow's crumbling importance and wanted to take control of more areas for themselves so they could replace the field mice as the Field's most important creatures. With all the confusion which had overtaken the Hedgerow as the field mice tried to solve their problems with the grey squirrels, rabbits and rats, the shrews believed their moment had arrived. Like others, the shrews also saw more creatures moving to the Rise and were jealous of this too. The Rise was becoming increasingly important as it swapped more and many creatures looked up to it. The shrews wanted this to stop. These things aside, the main reason the shrew leader, known as the Chancellor, wanted to fight was to distract the shrews. They were unhappy and felt the Chancellor was not doing enough to stop wanderers arriving in the Backwater.

The Chancellor, who had barged his way to power following the death of the last shrew Crown Prince only a few seasons before, was little known around the Field. Brushing his hair forwards to puff it out and make himself look bigger than the other shrews, the Chancellor had a voice which sounded like a tree branch snapping in the wind when he barked orders to his generals in the Backwater's army. For many seasons, even before he was leader, the Chancellor had been forming a grand plan in his mind for how the Backwater would become the Field's most important area. Now that moment had arrived, he was excited. With too few creatures and a small army, the Rise was unable to fill the void left by the Hedgerow, so there was room for another area to step in.

The Chancellor called all the shrews to the edge of the Backwater at dusk one summer's evening to tell them all about his grand plan. Standing in the middle of the Backwater on the tip of a slender canoe of finely woven reeds while his audience lined the banks, the Chancellor raised his forepaws in the air dramatically and the crowd's nattering died, leaving silence broken only by crickets chirping in the reeds. Waiting for a long moment or two, the Chancellor began passionately. 'Shrews are the purest and noblest of all creatures in the Field,' he cried before tailing off boredly, 'but you know this already...' Taking a moment to regain his composure, he launched again with renewed gusto. 'Now is our chance!' There was much applause at these simple words. 'We all know the field mice's problems. God has provided us shrews with the perfect opportunity to make ourselves the Field's most important creatures once and for all!'

Sharp, with few words wasted, this speech was strangely similar to the one the Queen had given many seasons before when she had called upon the field mice to think outside the hawthorns, sloes, elders and brambles of the Hedgerow to the Field beyond. That speech had finished with the Queen sharing her belief that the field mice were chosen by God to lead all creatures not as clever or capable as they.

Things had changed in the Field since then. Now it was not just the otters living on the Riverbank or the voles in the Watermeadow, there were different creatures living together in many areas, and the same was true for the Backwater. In his speech, by telling the shrews that they were the best of all creatures, the Chancellor had torn straight down the middle the special understanding which enabled many different creatures to live together in the Backwater. On one side were the shrews, excited by the opportunity to show they were the best, and on the other side were all the other creatures, like the grey squirrels, rats and rabbits who had joined the shrews in calling the Backwater home.

'How naïve these creatures are,' yelled the Chancellor from the canoe, 'coming to the Backwater and thinking that they can live here alongside us fine shrews. They are not the same as us, we are better!' The shrews on the bank jeered and the Chancellor continued, stirring up a frenzy. 'Our home is being taken from us. Before we can take up

God's call and show the rest of the Field how strong and clever we are, we must solve this problem!' Finishing his speech, the Chancellor threw his forepaws in the air in triumph. Surprising even him, the shrews along the edge of the Backwater did the same, shouting, cheering and rushing into the shallows to splash about in awe of their leader and his dream.

What a speech! Such passion and conviction! It would be remembered by the shrews for many seasons to come. In the days that followed, shrews of all shapes and sizes lined up to become soldiers in the Backwater's army, eager to help realise the Chancellor's vision. For those creatures living in the Backwater who were not shrews, things became unpleasant. The shrews now looked down their snouts at them, making snide remarks behind their paws and telling them they did not deserve to call the Backwater home. But this was only the beginning, though. Things got much worse, as they soon started having food and other things they had collected and made taken from their burrows while they were sleeping. But still, it did not stop here. Before long, things were being stolen in daylight too. These other creatures, getting angry and trying to stop this happening, were beaten, kicked, scratched and told that everything in the Backwater now belonged to shrews only. Not long after this, shrew soldiers went from burrow to burrow, arresting these creatures, old and young. Some were lucky, simply forced to rummage and forage, much like the rats and rabbits in the Hedgerow had been. Others were also lucky, forced to use the wood their peers collected to build big walls to protect the Backwater from attackers. But many were not so, taken by the army to huge burrows freshly dug far underground. Stories from these burrows never made their way to the surface. Once a creature was taken there, never again did the sun glint in their beady eyes.

Rumours of what happened in these burrows abounded in the Backwater. Some shrews thought they were connected to long passages leading to dens underneath the Briary where the foxes waited, eating the other creatures one by one as they tried to escape. Others thought they were taken to these burrows and the entrances then collapsed, burying them alive. Some shrews were less cynical. They thought the creatures were being kept underground, hidden from an attack on the Backwater, making swords, spears, shields and all the things the Backwater's army needed as it got bigger.

These rumours travelled quickly around the Field. While creatures from other areas did not like the sound of these stories, most felt the Backwater was too far away for them to really mean much. 'No badger has ever left the Sett and moved to the Backwater. It's on the opposite side of the Field, what does it have to do with us?' The badgers shrugged nonchalantly. Others, like the otters, who now did most of their swapping with the shrews, simply turned a blind eye, not wanting to ruin things for themselves. But mostly, the creatures from other areas, like the Warren and the Copse, were too weak and unorganised to do anything, even if they had wanted to. The horrible things the Chancellor was doing continued. Steadily, the Backwater got stronger as the shrews forced the other creatures to collect more things to swap and make more weapons. With more weapons, the army needed more soldiers to use them, so the army grew too.

Before long, the Chancellor felt a tickle in his big toe and knew the moment had come; the Backwater was now strong enough to rival the Hedgerow. When this happened, he quickly set in motion the next step of his plan. Early one bright summer morning, as the ducks paddled to the middle of the Backwater and took flight towards the Riverbank to spend the day splashing about looking for food, the Chancellor ordered the army to invade the Backwater's closest neighbours.

The dormice from the Brush and the hedgehogs from the Meadow were private creatures with little interest in the goings-on of others in the Field – they only had armies for fun parades in summer. Being small and with little in the way of food, wood and precious stones, having the Brush and Meadow did not give the shrews much of an advantage, but the Chancellor knew invading them would send a strong message to the Field's other creatures and he wanted them all to fear the shrews. No creature was safe from them.

Seeking help, the Chancellor visited the Watermeadow and Briary, promising the vole Sultan and fox Emperor lots of different things to encourage them to join the fighting with the Backwater. Jealous of the field mice and keen to become important too, the Sultan and Emperor agreed, their armies immediately helping the shrews to invade the Bottom Corner, some of the Warren and the rat's half of the Hedgerow. Being so close to the field mice, the Chancellor knew invading the rats would make the Queen and the new representatives angry. But there was still one final step in the Chancellor's plan to realise his dream. Long envious of the field mice, he wanted to take the Hedgerow from them too.

life difficult for the Chancellor and the shrew, vole and fox armies he now led, the Hedgerow had one big problem, and the Chancellor knew what it was. With most of their food coming from swapping with other areas, the field mice were reliant upon groups of creatures hauling heavily laden wooden sleds backwards and forwards across the Field to stop them going hungry.

One morning towards the end of summer, as the Chancellor walked around the edge of the Backwater to clear his head, he saw the ducks taking flight to the Riverbank for the day. If the ducks could not fly and leave the Backwater, the Chancellor thought, then they would starve; there was not enough food for them there. Maybe the Hedgerow was the same? He mused. There was no food there for the field mice anymore and, if they could not get it from other areas, maybe they would become like the ducks in a blizzard when it was too cold and windy to fly; maybe they would starve too. Realising this, the Chancellor became excited. If he could stop sleds going to the Hedgerow, the field mice would be cut off from the rest of the Field and they would no longer have food and many of the other things the Prime Minister and representatives needed to keep order and stay friendly with the other creatures they swapped with. Without any food, the field mice would quickly weaken, either surrendering or becoming an easy target for attack by the shrew, vole and fox armies.

To put his new plan into action, the Chancellor ordered his generals to form small bands of soldiers who hid next to the paths the sleds used, ready to jump from the lush grass and charge the unsuspecting haulers. No creature was spared, all those pulling the sleds quickly slaughtered before the soldiers disappeared back into the grass to wait for the next sled. As the Chancellor predicted, this became a big problem for the Hedgerow. To protect the haulers and their sleds, the number of field mice soldiers travelling with them had to rival the number of attackers, and there were many sleds and even more shrew, vole and fox soldiers. The Hedgerow simply did not have enough soldiers to make sure every sled was safe. Many were lost.

Instead of eating as much as they wanted, whenever they wanted, with less food, the field mice were only allowed a little every now and again. As this morsel got steadily smaller, the soldiers defending the Hedgerow practised their fighting less and fell asleep in the crooks of high branches when they were meant to be on watch. But it was not only the army, the other field mice were also hungry. As more haulers and soldiers – family and friends – were killed, they got very upset. The more upset they got, the more they grumbled among themselves, some even saying they should surrender to the shrews. They would rather be ruled by the Chancellor and have a full tummy than be hungry and free…

Word of yet another attacked sled made its way back to the Hedgerow late one bitter winter's afternoon, as the frost settled over the Field like a big sheet of the silky cloth the field mice had once woven, smothering happiness. Something needed to be done and a general in the field mice army had an idea. Although very clever, the idea was an unpopular headache for all the creatures organising the pulling and guarding of the sleds, but still the general persisted. Instead of leaving whenever the haulers felt like it, his idea was for the sleds to wait and then leave in a big group, guarded at the front, sides and back by the burliest of the Hedgerow army's soldiers.

The Chancellor's tactics were thwarted. Instead of picking off almost every sled, the bands of shrews, voles and foxes could only wait in hiding and get one or two sleds as the long groups passed by and the field mouse soldiers retaliated. This was a turning point in the Hedgerow's fortunes against the shrews and the general became very well-known and a close friend of the Queen (a dream for many field mice). This brought a new wave of confidence to the Hedgerow. The field mice felt that they could be as strong as they had been all those seasons before and would not be defeated by the Backwater, Watermeadow and Briary.

Although the flow of things to and from the Hedgerow continued, it remained under siege for many seasons more, the shrews, voles and foxes lurking just out sight of the field mice sentries, ready to pounce. But they were never able to; the Chancellor had underestimated attacking the Hedgerow.

The field mice soldiers, unlike those from other areas, had had a lot of practice fighting in recent seasons, and the army's generals had a response for every challenge the Chancellor threw at them. Even more so, the Hedgerow's soldiers had experience with the bloody bit of fighting, which most creatures did not. They had killed and seen their friends killed; death was nothing new to them.

As the seasons rolled through carelessly one after the other, much as the clouds roll endlessly across the sky delivering sun, rain and life, the resilience of the field mice was eventually rewarded as the enthusiasm of the Chancellor's siege weakened. Realising invading the Hedgerow was taking up most of the soldiers, weapons and spirit of the shrew, vole and fox armies, the Chancellor turned his attention to the easier but less exciting places he could invade on the other side of the Field. Mostly large but weak, until now these areas had played little role in changing things in the Field, swapping little and avoiding making friends with creatures from other areas.

Once again, the Chancellor was wrong. The ferrets were overcome quickly but the beavers from the Brook put up a hard fight, taking back some of the Thicket for their ferret neighbours. The beavers' retaliation kept the best divisions of the vole army engaged in fighting that went on endlessly through one of the coldest winters in memory. Seeing this, the water rats from the Spring, which trickled down the side of the Field into the River, flew a white flag of surrender before any blood was shed. They then started a secret resistance movement in an attempt to bring the invading shrews down from the inside.

The unexpected resilience from the areas the Chancellor thought would be easy to beat required more soldiers and weapons than he had available, even with the Watermeadow and Briary's armies. Spread across multiple areas and having to quickly train inexperienced soldiers to replace the rapidly growing number of dead and wounded, the Chancellor's grand dream began to crumble.

22

Protecting the sleds travelling across the Field had foiled the Chancellor's plan, but still he kept trying to attack. Through sheer persistence, the shrew, vole and fox armies started to succeed, but it was too late, it made no difference to his failing dream. Losing fights with the creatures they tried to invade, including many they should have won easily, the shrew generals began to lose faith in the Chancellor and took matters into their own paws. Ignoring his orders, the generals' tactics became reckless, being less selective of the groups of sleds they ambushed travelling to the Hedgerow. This was a big mistake.

One late autumn afternoon, as a light breeze plucked the remaining leaves from the Hedgerow and sent them twirling across the Field with the elegance of the finest rabbit dancers, a band of shrew soldiers lay in the damp grass beside the busiest path to the Hedgerow. Waiting impatiently, the soldiers pulled their jackets tighter around themselves to keep out the cold. They soon felt the familiar rumble of a group of sleds through their bellies, starting as a mere tickle and getting stronger and stronger. The captain of the band popped his head up quickly to see where the sleds were travelling. Getting closer, the shrew soldiers heard the voices of the haulers.

The shrew captain had seen all he needed to. The group of sleds were heading towards the Hedgerow and neither as long nor guarded by as many soldiers as usual. The creatures hauling them were also not from the Hedgerow. He did not recognise the colourful jackets the soldiers wore, but it did not matter; the sleds were taking food to the Hedgerow and he had orders to do as much damage to the sleds and kill as many creatures as possible.

The captain did not realise these sleds were from the Rise, which had played no part in the fighting so far. Many creatures who now called the Rise home had fled fighting and could not bear the thought of more. On the other paw, the creatures of the Rise were cunning and saw an opportunity to benefit from the disarray: as each area involved in the fighting grew their armies, there were more soldiers than ever before and far fewer creatures collecting or making things.

The Rise swapped things with all areas. Even after hearing rumours of the horrible things the Chancellor was doing to those creatures in the Backwater who were not shrews, the President did not stop swapping with the shrews, voles and foxes. Having to defend themselves from the Chancellor's armies, which required more food and more weapons, the Rise stepped in to help these other areas, like the Hedgerow. To do this, the creatures from the Rise formed their own groups of haulers and soldiers to drag things across the

Field, including to the Hedgerow. Spending every waking moment fighting or defending, the field mice could neither collect nor make things to swap with the Rise in return for the things it gave them. This mattered little to the President: he knew the fighting might go on for many seasons, but it would certainly not go on forever. He also knew it was not just the Hedgerow; many other areas needed help too. So, he offered these areas a different sort of swapping than had been done before. Instead of directly swapping one thing for another at once, as was usually the case, the Rise now swapped things but received nothing in return when the swapping took place, doing so on the condition things would be given back to them in seasons to come.

What was in it for the creatures of the Rise? How did they know they were going to receive things for what they had already swapped? The President had a clever idea to solve this problem. The amount the Rise expected creatures to swap back would increase with each season. If the Rise swapped a basket of berries for a bundle of wood from the Hedgerow but the field mice could not provide the bundle straight away, then the next season they would have to swap back two bundles instead of one. If they could still not swap it back, in another two seasons the amount would grow by another two bundles, making it four for the one basket of berries, long eaten and forgotten. Because the areas the Rise was swapping with were both big and small and had different things the Rise wanted and lesser or greater chances of being able to swap them back, the amounts the Rise expected each area to swap in return differed as well. The badgers, who had lots of delicious nuts to swap, would only have to swap back two nuts extra per season for every ten they still needed to give the Rise. On the other paw, the grey squirrels, with the very few silky pods they still had to offer, had to swap back five extra pods per season for every ten they owed the Rise. Knowing the grey squirrels would take longer to swap back the things they owed, the President thought it only fair the Rise take more from them. Still, these creatures had no choice. As the fighting carried on for many seasons, the number of things some of them needed to swap back grew immensely. Realising the benefit of this new type of swapping to the Rise in seasons to come, the President instructed more sleds be made so the Rise could haul more things to swap across the Field.

It was one of these groups the shrew captain now saw. Getting closer, the shrew soldiers drew their wooden swords and the captain whispered, 'On the ready.' There was a pause. 'CHARGE!'

23

The haulers and soldiers from the Rise were caught by surprise! Up until then, the shrew, vole and fox armies had always recognised their sleds and avoided attacking them. The swapping these areas did with the Rise had been essential for helping them through the fighting. Being peaceful creatures with little experience in paw-to-paw combat, the soldiers from the Rise were quickly overcome and they, and the haulers, suffered quick, brutal deaths from the shrews' swords. The shrew soldiers, suffering only a pawful of cuts and bruises, celebrated by jumping up and down in glee, hugging each other and brandishing their weapons and flags in the air. This was the Backwater's first victory in the fighting for many moons. There was now a glint of hope for these soldiers: maybe they could weaken the Hedgerow and stop the sleds one by one?

What a mistake these shrews had made. Word of the slaughter travelled quickly back to the Rise from the Hedgerow, where field mouse soldiers on lookout in the topmost branches had seen the saga take place but were too far away to do anything. The President heard about it first. He told his generals, who told their captains, who told their soldiers, who passed it on to their families and friends. Before long, every creature in the Rise had heard about it and were upset. They were not taking sides in the fighting, the Rise was swapping with all creatures. Why would the Chancellor target them?

The creatures of the Rise were proud of what they had achieved in only a few seasons. They were proud of how they had become so important in the swapping, and how creatures from all over the Field who had fled fighting and hardship wanted to join their home: somewhere they could live peacefully and be treated the same whether they were a field mouse, grey squirrel, mole, rabbit or rat. For this reason, they took the attack personally. It was not just an attack on a group of sleds bound for the Hedgerow, it was an attack on the Rise, the things it stood for and the creatures who called it home.

As had happened in other areas before, the creatures gathered below the President's palace in the sweet-smelling cedar tree. From the rolling-thunder bellowing of the otters to the squeaky squeals of the dormice and everything in between, the creatures stayed there yelling in complaint as loudly as they could. The sun and moon swapped places in the sky again and again until the President realised that something needed to be done.

'If the stories are true about what the Chancellor has been doing to the creatures of the Backwater who are not shrews, something must be done,' the President announced earnestly to the creatures gathered below from his perch on a slender cedar branch glistening silver like the Spring trickling in the summer sun. 'Regrettably, we will join the fighting on the side of the Hedgerow, Warren, Thicket, Brook, Meadow and other areas the Backwater, Watermeadow and Briary have turned against. With our friends we will bring down our new enemies, making the Field a more peaceful place than it has ever been before.'

The crowd breathed a sigh of relief. They were going to stand up for all the things they believed in and do something to help their fellow creatures and protect their pride. With many areas still having lots of things they had promised to swap back later when they had them, the Rise found it had become very powerful. The President travelled the Field, reminding the leaders of these areas before asking them to help the Rise in the fighting. Owing much to the Rise, there was only one thing they could do in response: offering all the help they could. In the days following the President's speech, many passionate creatures joined the Rise's army and, with lots of things to swap, the Rise had the best weapons for these soldiers to fight with.

The armies of the Backwater, Watermeadow and Briary were tired of fighting. For many seasons they had seen friends die. When the President sent a message on a curl of cedar bark to the Chancellor explaining that the Rise was joining the fighting against them, the Chancellor passed it to his generals, the vole Sultan and the fox Emperor. As soldiers from the three armies heard this message, they could do little but sit down, put their heads in their forepaws and weep. They knew how big the Rise was, how many things it had to swap and the weapons that this would bring to

24

Things were not matching the Chancellor's promises to the fox Emperor, so he decided the fighting was lost and surrendered to the Rise to save the lives of the remaining soldiers in his army. The Chancellor was furious when he heard, ordering his generals to turn against the fox soldiers, capturing them and forcing them to make more weapons, build fences and dig ditches to help the Backwater. The shrew army was weak and its soldiers unhappy, so most of the generals ignored the Chancellor, fearing their soldiers would turn against them as well. This made the President of the Rise happy. He ordered his generals to lead the captured fox soldiers back to the Briary and keep them there, making sure their weapons were collected and destroyed so no fox could leave and go back to fighting for the Chancellor.

Not long after, the Sultan of the voles did the same thing for the very same reason. Once again, the President of the Rise ordered his generals to march the vole soldiers back to the Watermeadow and destroy their weapons. He then set about making use of the vole soldiers, telling his generals to force them to start collecting and making things the Watermeadow could swap back for the things they owed to the Rise which they had taken during the many seasons of fighting.

Once again, the Chancellor saw his dream of a Field ruled by the shrews collapsing around him and issued orders to his generals to make sure the shrew soldiers would not surrender like the treacherous foxes and voles. 'We will keep fighting to the end,' he told them. 'The soldiers of the Rise, Hedgerow and Warren have become complacent. Now is the opportunity to attack!' But the shrew soldiers no longer cared; they had had enough. They wanted things to return to the way they had been before the fighting. The Backwater was big and there had always been enough space, food and reeds for building nests before the fighting. Why did the Chancellor want more? Why had he made them want more? How many of their fellow creatures would die trying to realise his dream? Why had he not learnt from the field mouse Queen who had wanted much the same thing? Look where the field mice were now: they were getting stronger since being driven from the Copse all those seasons ago. Teamed with the Rise, they were now beating the shrews. The shrew soldiers wondered, if they gave in like the foxes and voles, would things go back to being the same for them? Was there anything to be gained from more fighting?

These questions were discussed in intense whispers as the shrew soldiers sharpened their sturdy wooden swords, waiting for the call to leap up and charge the soldiers from the Rise, Hedgerow and Warren waiting patiently for them.

They discussed them as they scraped shallow graves for their friends, and as they lay shivering in silent drizzle trying to sleep with the fear a field mouse, weasel or rabbit would appear out of the darkness, pointing a spear at their heart.

The shrew generals heard these whispers and started asking the same questions themselves. Like their soldiers, they had had enough too. At the beginning of the fighting seasons before, the Chancellor had promised them it would not last long and that, when they won, each of them would have their own invaded area to rule as they pleased. This had not happened. They had been away from the Backwater and their families for many seasons and were tired of carrying out the Chancellor's plans for him, most of which they disagreed with.

So, after many nights of whispered discussions, the generals did it; they stopped urging their soldiers to fight harder. They stopped promising them wonderful things after the fighting when the Backwater had won. And they stopped picking up swords themselves and leading raids on the camps of soldiers from the Rise, Hedgerow and Warren in the dead of night. When this happened, the fighting took its last turn and the armies led by the Rise pushed closer towards the Backwater.

The Chancellor heard them coming, the impatient clattering and screaming of battle getting closer and closer until he could bear it no more. He knew the Backwater had lost; he had lost. Soon the soldiers from the Rise would be there and he would be captured. They would find out the truth about what had happened to the creatures he had sent underground. They might kill him – that was if the shrews, when they realised what he had led them into, did not get him first.

He decided to end it all before they came. Carrying a small, sharp sword, he took his final walk to the end of a secret tunnel the shrews had dug in case they ever needed to flee the Backwater to the Briary for safety. The tunnel was useless now. He could save himself the embarrassment of surrendering and the pain of all the horrible things they might do to him. Down the end of this tunnel he could disappear and only the worms would know where he had gone. Secrets were safe with them; they shared nothing with the other creatures.

But no creature could ever truly disappear. The stories that filled the memories of all the Field's creatures combined were stronger and lasted far longer than anything scrawled on a dried chestnut leaf in mulberry juice ink. These memories were stronger than a shrew with its paws tied, dragged through every area in the Field, looking each creature in the eye that they had affected trying to realise their dream. They were stronger than the body of a dead shrew, hung up for all to see and jeer at. They were stronger than a shrew locked away in a dark burrow somewhere for the rest of their days. And they were stronger than a piece of flat river stone, half buried on its edge to mark where the body of a shrew lay. No matter where he went or what he did, the Field's creatures, both now and for many seasons to come, would know of the Chancellor of the Shrews. They would know of his failed dream and how it had changed the Field forever in ways he had never imagined.

25

Although the Chancellor had gone, the message of what had happened in the Backwater took a while to reach some of the far-flung areas where the shrew army was still strong, so the fighting continued for a pawful more moons. Upon hearing of the Chancellor's disappearance, one shrew general tried to move the home of the shrews to the Furrow where the stoats lived, one of the Field's smallest areas. Fleeing the Backwater before soldiers from the Rise, Hedgerow and Warren turned up, upon arriving in the Furrow, the general quickly proclaimed himself the new Chancellor of the Shrews. Gathering his soldiers and their families about him, he sent a message to the President of the Rise declaring the Furrow to be the new home of the shrews and he the leader of free creatures that would fight hard to keep it that way.

Hearing this message, the President laughed. The Furrow was tiny and his generals reported that there were only a few score shrew soldiers guarding it. He ordered this new 'Chancellor' be captured to end his plans before they became a problem. He need not have worried: the stoats beat him to it, turning on the shrews that had brutally taken their home and killing every last one.

One by one, the shrew generals and their armies holding different bits of the Field lay down their weapons, threw their paws in the air and walked out from behind the bushes, fences and ditches where they hid. They came out from behind the dreams and promises of the old Chancellor and into horrible reality. The Backwater was leaderless, captured and embarrassed for all the things it had done.

Just as with the foxes and voles, soldiers from the Rise quickly marched the shrew soldiers back to the Backwater, which was now controlled by generals from the Rise, Hedgerow and Warren. While this was happening, a meeting of all the leaders and generals on both sides of the fighting was held. At this meeting, it was agreed that the shrews would return all the areas they had invaded to the creatures whose homes they had been before. They also agreed to get rid of their army so they could not fight again; the Rise, Hedgerow and Warren promising to defend them if any creatures ever tried to invade the Backwater. Finally, the shrews reluctantly agreed to give most of the things they would collect and make in the coming seasons to the creatures they had fought, making up for all these creatures had lost. The shrews were unhappy about this. The fruits of their efforts for many seasons to come would be taken from them to make up for what the now-dead Chancellor had done. It did not seem fair: why should they bear the burden of their old Chancellor's crazy ideas; they had not been their ideas?

It took a few seasons for the shrews to come to terms with losing the fighting. When they finally did, they were embarrassed at what had happened and how blindly they had followed the Chancellor. None of this mattered to the creatures who had fought against the shrews, voles and foxes. Their homes, families, friends and many things they had collected and made had been taken from them. Giving back even a little of this was the least the shrews could do.

To make up for this loss, the shrews needed to collect and make twice as many things – a challenge – but it is exactly what they did.

26

After the agreement to end the fighting was signed, things in the Field did not go back to the way they were before. Scared the shrews might suddenly return to their horrible ways, the President made sure the Rise, Hedgerow and Warren kept soldiers in the Backwater to keep an eye on them and help choose a new Chancellor. Once again, this angered the shrews, but they could do nothing; they had no army, they could not retaliate. They could stop collecting and making things and gather together in a big group and shout and yell, but the President of the Rise would not listen. It was just best to get on with things.

Even though the shrews, voles and foxes were under control, the creatures from the Field's other areas were still worried fighting would break out again. Feeling this nervousness, the President decided to call a big meeting. The first of its kind in the Field, the leaders of every area were invited to the Rise to discuss what should be done. The areas worst affected by the fighting had little food and their nests and burrows were crumbling. The President wanted to discuss how the Field's bigger areas not so badly affected by the fighting could help them. With the Rise swapping many things with lots of areas during the fighting but receiving nothing in return, the President realised that it would take a long while for these creatures to swap back the things they had agreed to seasons before. He thought this needed solving too.

There were three problems to discuss and the President had some ideas for ways all the creatures could band together to solve them. It was going to be difficult; never before had all the creatures in the Field agreed on something like this, but the President thought it was possible.

27

Much was changing in the Warren too. Although the rabbits had beaten the shrews, they were unhappy with their new tsar. Returning with his family from the Divet, the rabbits were initially excited to have their leader back. They were proud to have a tsar, and of all the things the rabbits had ever done, remembering all the good bits, like regaining their freedom from the field mice, and forgetting most of the bad, like the strange sickness. Upon the Tsar's return to the Warren, the rabbits began to see things were not as they remembered. While he was undoubtedly a rabbit, the Tsar acted and spoke like a hare, and he had never so much as led a picnic party, let alone a whole Warren. When there was a particularly chilly winter and little food, the Tsar did not know what to do. Should he try and swap more things for food with the other creatures? Should he tell the rabbits to collect different types of food? None of his advisors knew either. They had never really done anything other than collect and make things for the field mice; freedom was something completely different.

The Tsar always had enough food and lived in the biggest burrow in the Warren decorated with special stones, so it did not matter to him; his life went on. He had faith the rabbit god who had brought him back to the Warren would solve these problems for him. But the god did not and the problems stayed. The rabbits were frustrated, complaining loudly that they were ruled by a hare who did know what he was doing and cared little for the rabbits. They were not wrong.

When the shrews had started trying to invade the Warren, strangely the Tsar had become excited. He had heard rumours of what his rabbit subjects were saying about him and thought the invasion would be an opportunity to distract them and allow him to prove himself as their leader. As the shrews frantically tried to dig their way into the Warren, the Tsar had lain lay on his back in the Warren's biggest burrow daydreaming of leading the rabbits into the fighting and winning. If the rabbits won, he had thought, he could take some of the Backwater and rule more of the Field, more creatures and become much more important.

Things were never as simple as that in the Field. While the first bit of his plan went well, the rabbits becoming distracted from the harsh winter and lack of food, the second bit did not and the creatures in the Warren liked him no more. They were not fighting for him; they were fighting for themselves and their freedom. Locked away in his burrow with his family, the Tsar had not realised, he thought everything was going very well indeed.

The shrews had steadily pushed into the Warren, taking some of the smaller burrows, but the rabbits had stood their ground, many willing to die defending their home. Whenever another burrow was lost, the Tsar and his family had visited the soldiers. Strolling through their tired and grubby ranks, the Tsar had grasped each by the paw and told them all the creatures in the Warren were very proud of what they were doing. His family had given them extra warm jackets to keep out the chill of the winter nights and the soldiers would smile weakly in thanks, cursing them and spitting on the ground after they had left. The Tsar and his family did not know what it was like to be a real rabbit and fight. They had never looked death in the beady shrew eye or had an empty tummy and cold paws.

This sentiment continued throughout the fighting as the shrew army invaded more of the Warren and the rabbit soldiers got angrier. On the day the rogue band of shrew soldiers raided the Rise's sleds heading to the Hedgerow, everything had changed.

When the Rise joined the fighting, the President had split his army so it could fight the shrews, voles and foxes in the different parts of the Field they were trying to invade. Having taken the Brush from the dormice and the Meadow from the hedgehogs on one side of the Field, the Chancellor had thought invading the Warren on the Field's other side would be important, taking him closer to the Hedgerow. Many soldiers from the shrew army were sent there, but when the Rise joined the fighting, the Chancellor suddenly had to take soldiers from areas where there were many and send them to areas where there were few. With the shrew army vastly outnumbered in the Warren, the rabbits had been able to drive them out for good and, alongside soldiers from the Rise and Hedgerow, start pushing towards the Backwater.

The Tsar, the young, naïve buck that he was, thought this had been his doing. In his eyes, his leadership had won the fighting and now the Warren was one of the most important areas in the Field and he one of its most important creatures. Having sided with the Rise and Hedgerow to defeat the Backwater, the Tsar had joined the President, Prime Minister and remaining shrew generals in putting his pawprint on the agreement that had ended the fighting.

The rest of the rabbits did not see it this way, they saw it for what it was: the Warren had only beaten the Backwater because of the Rise. The fighting had left the Warren in a mess. Before retreating, shrew soldiers had collapsed burrows they had invaded, and having been so busy fighting, many other parts of the Warren had not been looked after, left to crumble and cave in. The Warren also owed the Rise many things in return for what they had swapped during the fighting and, with the death of many rabbits during the shrew's invasion, there were now not nearly as many creatures to collect and make things to swap back. Seasons rolled by and more and more they owed. It looked as if they may never swap everything back.

Like the other problems, the rabbits expected the Tsar to lead them, but he did not know what to do. Just as was happening in many other areas when creatures became unhappy, the rabbits gathered together, shouting for something to happen. The Tsar ignored them, hoping the problem would go away. When it did not and more and more rabbits shouted and banged on the entrance to his burrow, he did the only thing he could think of and sent soldiers to make them go away. It was a mistake killing hungry rabbits who only wanted their burrows to be rebuilt made them angrier.

The rebellious group that had led the rabbits to freedom from the Hedgerow all those seasons before still existed. These rabbits, seeing the Tsar was not fit to lead the Warren, waited patiently, as they had before, for the day they could become truly free – free in the sense that all creatures living in the Warren would be treated the same, just like the Rise. But there the similarities with the Rise stopped. The rebellious rabbits' idea of freedom was very different.

In the Rise, each creature was free to have their own burrow and more food and other things if they put effort into collecting and making it themselves. The rebellious rabbits thought freedom meant more than this. They thought being free and being the same meant that all the Warren's burrows and all the food and other things the rabbits made and collected should be evenly divided among the creatures living there. Only by having the same amount of everything would creatures be truly free and treated the same. But they went even further than this, extending their idea from how the Warren should be organised to how decisions were made. Instead of having one leader who made the final decision on everything, the rebels thought special groups should be formed to discuss and make decisions on different things, a bit like the rats had tried. To make sure as many creatures as possible were involved in deciding what should happen in the Warren, each group would make a recommendation to another above them that discussed it and made a recommendation to another group for another decision. This would happen until the final recommendation reached the last and most important group who made the final decision.

The rebels thought they had come up with a fantastic way of organising themselves. A way by which all rabbits could be truly free, treated the same and benefit from the effort every creature in the Warren put into collecting, making and doing all the things they needed to. Most excitingly, though, they believed that this way would allow all the creatures in the Warren to help make decisions. The logic was, that by involving as many creatures as possible, the best decisions would be made and one leader would be stopped from doing whatever they wanted, like the shrew Chancellor. Or so they thought.

After the Tsar sent his soldiers to stop the rabbits shouting outside his burrow, the rebels finally saw their chance. For those rabbits still unsure about the Tsar, this was the turning point. How could they defend a leader who turned soldiers on his own creatures? Secretly, the rebels met with generals in the Warren's army, asking them why they still fought for the Tsar and explaining their new plan for the Warren. The generals had little respect for the Tsar either; they hated having to turn their soldiers on the creatures they were meant to be protecting. When the rebels promised the generals that they and their army would be important in the Warren once their plan was realised and the Tsar no more, the generals thought long and hard, realising proudly that the only reason the Tsar was still tsar was because they were defending him. The power was in their paws; they could change the Warren forever. Liking this idea, they agreed to join the rebels.

Late one overcast autumn night, as the clouds threatened to relieve themselves suddenly of the rain they carried, the generals and their soldiers, led by the rebel ringleaders, stormed the Tsar's burrow, capturing him and his family. There was nothing the Tsar could do; his army had turned against him. Roughly covering the heads of the Tsar and his family with thick bags woven from rough grass and usually used for carrying golden nuggets, the soldiers carried them away to a hidden burrow on the edge of the Warren.

While this was happening, the rebels and generals started forming lots of groups to begin making decisions in the Warren. Decisions like: what should happen to the Tsar and his family? Should they be allowed to go back to the Divet to live with the hares? Should they be locked away in a burrow forever? Or should they be killed, wiping away their memory and preventing them from ever trying to lead the Warren again? Such was the hardship the rabbits had faced since the Tsar's return, it was an easy decision. The Tsar and his family were killed secretly in the middle of the night by a small band of the roughest, toughest rabbit soldiers who only answered to the rebel ringleader, the self-appointed Chair-rabbit of the Warren's biggest and most important group for making decisions.

All this happened so quickly, few of the Field's other creatures saw it coming. Immediately, the Chair-rabbit and all the new groups set about organising the rebuilding of the Warren and the collecting and making of things to swap back to the Rise. The rabbits were proud of this; they had taken control of their home and believed that they were the first area in the Field where all creatures were truly treated the same. Everything collected or made was shared; no creature could have more than another.

This gave the rabbits confidence. So many seasons had been spent ruled by creatures who cared little for them. Now the shrews were defeated and the Field was a different place, could they spread their new way of organising themselves to other areas of the Field, offering the same freedom they now had? If so, maybe these places would look to the Warren for guidance? Maybe – just maybe – it could become the Field's most important area and control the swapping of things. Many of the new groups for making decisions discussed this at great length and the Chair-rabbit gave many speeches to the bands of rabbits formed to collect and make different things for all in the Warren to share. These rabbits excitedly chattered about it. What a wonderful idea it was; finally they might become important!

Only one thing stood in the Warren's way of realising this dream. Before the fighting had broken out, this had been the very same dream of the President of the Rise too. Now the fighting was over and the Field was a very different place, the President thought he should put his plan into action. The big meeting at the Rise to which all the Field's leaders were invited was the beginning of this.

28

On the morning of the big meeting of all the Field's areas, the President declared that all creatures in the Rise should have a day away from collecting and making things to welcome the leaders. What a spectacle it was! The Prime Minister of the Hedgerow arrived, followed by a pawful of his most loyal representatives. Looking sombre in neat, dark jackets, they knew the meeting would be a momentous occasion for the Field and were nervous, but still managed to wave to the thronging crowds. The leaders of the Brook and the Thicket arrived next, each flanked by their beaver and ferret soldiers carrying spears twice the height of themselves with red, blue, green and yellow flags flying from their tips. After them was the Chair-rabbit, escorted on either side by his own band of the roughest, toughest rabbit soldiers wearing nothing but grimaces. The moles followed, travelling the only way they knew how and arriving with a gentle rumble and spray of earth as their tunnel from the Bottom Corner broke through and the beady eyes and dirty nose of the mole King popped out. Not wanting to be outdone, the hares turned up in a swirling cloud of dust the creatures of the Rise had seen bowling towards them from the Divet for most of the day as the hares bounded along, hoping not to be late. The otter elders entered the Rise to the beating of a hollow willow drum, singing moving songs about how much they already missed the River in their deep, treacly voices. And the hedgehog Pontiff shuffled in nervously, sporting the look of a creature unsure why they had been invited. His purple robes dragged behind him on the ground and a big crown of the brightest robin breast feathers sat atop his prickly head.

The creatures of the Rise lined the path to the President's cedar tree, cheering and waving in welcome as each leader arrived. Although creatures from all over the Field called the Rise home, it was the first many had seen of some of the creatures who lived in faraway corners of the Field and kept to themselves, like the adders, slithering past with their heads held high, or the spiders, scurrying here and there, their faces expressionless. The youngest creatures held their parents' paws, speechless. Were there really creatures without fur, ears and tails like them?

Upon arriving, the leaders bid goodbye to the soldiers and advisors who had accompanied them, making their way up the shimmering silver trunk of the cedar tree to the President's palace. Gathering in a big circle, the President stood in the middle of the leaders with his paws clasped on his belly. He reminded them all how monumental it was that creatures from every area in the Field were in one place together. Some leaders clapped and cheered; others, like the otters and beavers, sat quietly. They hated being up a tree, so far from water, and just wanted to get back to their River and Brook.

The meeting went on for a dozen moons – much longer than expected. Beginning every day just after dawn, it continued on long into the night, well after the sun had finished crossing the sky and the winking moon had taken its place. With little rest, the leaders discussed what they could do to stop fighting happening in the Field ever again, and ways areas needing to swap things back to the Rise after the fighting could do so. Finally, they spoke about how the areas left worse off by the fighting, having lost the most soldiers and had the most burrows and nests destroyed, could be helped.

The discussions went to, fro and around in circles as the leaders argued with one another, trying to get the best agreement for their area. The President naturally led proceedings, presenting the thing he thought needed changing and then giving the leaders the chance to offer their thoughts on the best way of doing so. This went on and on until the best ways of solving the problem were agreed upon.

Not all went as smoothly as it sounds. Most creatures disagreed with one another. Many stormed out of the meeting when they did not get their own way, only to return after the President found them sulking in a nearby prickle bush. He reassured them that they would get some of what they wanted, reminding them that they were taking part in shaping the Field for many seasons to come.

At the end of the final day, the exhausted President proudly stood to announce that the leaders had agreed on ways to solve the three problems he thought needed fixing. Opening his mouth to tell them this, his whiskers stiffened and the tiredness in his eyes disappeared instantly, replaced by the intensity of a confident creature inspiring those around them. 'Firstly,' he boomed to the leaders surrounding him, 'we have agreed that a special group will be made and that all areas will appoint a representative to it. This group will make a set of rules that all areas in the Field will follow and it will meet regularly in the Brush to make sure all creatures are following these rules. The Brush is the Field's smallest area and home to the dormice, who have never taken sides with any creatures and are well-liked.' There was polite applause from most of the leaders. Basing this group in such a small area with neither friends nor enemies meant creatures from the bigger areas, like the Hedgerow, Warren, Backwater and Rise, could not be upset that another important area was home to the group making the most important decisions and try to influence these decisions to suit themselves.

The President continued, 'Second, the Rise will change most of the swapping agreements we made with many areas during the fighting. Many creatures will never be able to give back all they have swapped with us. We have all agreed to lower the amounts that they have to swap back to make it easier for them to do so.' To help this, the President announced another group would be made, also based in the Brush with representatives from all areas. 'Each of the areas least impacted by the fighting will give some of their food and wood to this group, who will then give it to the areas they think were worst affected by the fighting.'

Finally, the President announced the creation of a third

group. 'Just like the other two, this group will help areas rebuild what was destroyed in the fighting. To do this, each area will offer their best builders, burrowers and advisors to areas finding things difficult.' Under the guidance of the President himself, this group would not only re-dig collapsed burrows and mend broken nests, but make sure each area had good creatures to lead it. For the President, a good leader meant one that all creatures in an area had agreed upon. And, just like him, he believed a good leader should make sure all creatures were treated the same, able to have their own things and never be scared that another creature might some day take these away from them.

The President was proud of this last group. He believed that the Rise's success was because of its good leaders in seasons past and that all areas should be just like it. This was the grand plan he had had before the fighting and, having waited patiently, he was now able to put it into action with the other leaders' approval. Like the Queen and Chancellor before him, the President felt that he had been chosen to make the Field a better place. He was the one who would bring peace and happiness. He was the one who would make sure all creatures could choose who led them, and that all the things they collected and made throughout their lives belonged to them and could not be taken away.

29

While most leaders in the meeting agreed on the first two groups, many disagreed with the last. Each area had a different way of choosing a leader and making decisions, and they thought their way was the best. Some leaders saw the President's push to create the final group for what it was: a way for the Rise to make more areas just like itself. Others, like the Chair-rabbit, thought that the President wanted the same thing that the Queen and Chancellor had wanted before him: to have power and control over the whole Field. The less sceptical, like the hedgehog Pontiff from the Meadow, thought that the President simply wanted the final group because he considered the Rise to be the best and believed the only way all other creatures in the Field would ever be happy was to do as they did.

Still, just like the Chair-rabbit, the Pontiff disagreed with what the President was doing. He thought the President had failed to see that, although some areas were bigger, others had more things and some were more inviting to wanderers; each was different, for both the right and wrong reasons. Each wore different-coloured jackets, spoke different-sounding languages, and collected and made different things. Each had a different way of finding a leader, a different name to call them and a different way of making decisions. And each of these differences was always changing. No area had always been that way. The Queen's family had not always been and would not always be rulers of the Hedgerow. The otters had not always called the Riverbank home and the beavers had not always built their dams on the Brook. The creatures were always moving from area to area, changing who led them. Sometimes this happened in a few seasons, like the rabbits who had gone from being ruled by the Queen, then the Tsar and now had a chair-rabbit. Sometimes it happened very slowly, as with the badgers from the Great Elm – no creature could recall them ever having been different, but many suspected that they probably had been once.

While the leaders unhappy with the final group cried in protest as the President made the announcement, there was nothing they could do. Suspecting many leaders would disagree with it, the President made sure all three decisions came together, the leaders only needing to add their pawprints to just one agreement on a dried chestnut leaf.

Exhausted from many moons of meetings, all the Field's leaders quickly added their pawprints to the agreement before gathering their advisors and soldiers and heading home. All, that is, except for a few leaders of the smallest areas that kept to themselves, like the adders and spiders, who cared little for the goings-on in the Field. And, most importantly, the Chair-rabbit and the leaders of the areas who did most of their swapping with the Warren. While others lined up to place their pawprints on the agreement, these leaders simply left the President's palace, clambering down the cedar tree and leaving the Rise.

Although he did not realise it, only wanting the best for the Field after the horrors of the fighting, the President had torn the invisible fabric the Field was suspended upon. Like most tears, slowly but surely it got longer and wider, splitting the creatures down the middle. On one side were those who had signed the agreement, supporting the President and the Rise. On the other were those supporting the Chair-rabbit and the Warren. The fighting was over in the Field for now, but there was a new rivalry.

30

When the Chair-rabbit arrived back in the Warren, he immediately set about discussing plans with the other members of the most important group. If the President was going to form new groups to help areas choose their leaders and make decisions in the same way as the Rise, the Warren would do the same thing too. In his passionate, eagerly beating rabbit heart, the Chair-rabbit knew most of the Field's leaders had only added their pawprints to the President's agreement in the hope that they would not have to swap back as many things with the Rise and that there would never again be fighting in the Field.

'These other creatures are not agreeing at all,' he told the other members of the most important group sternly. 'These other creatures are being only doing it for themselves.' His heart beat faster and he passionately began to shout. 'It is most unfair that the Rise can be telling these other creatures and us how to be organising ourselves and the type of leader we should be having. These other areas must be choosing what they are wanting to be doing!' He paused to catch a quick breath. 'The Warren will be helping these creatures who are wanting to be having a choice. If they are being given the choice,' he mused thoughtfully, his voice growing faint and whimsical, 'these creatures of course will be wanting to follow us. They will of course be wanting to have a Chair-creature – like me – and lots and lots and lots of groups to be sharing the making of decisions among as many creatures as is possibly possible!'

The members of the most important group made some humming noises and nodded their heads in agreement; of course the other areas would want every creature to be equal and have the same amount of everything. 'What is there not to be liking about this?' the Chair-rabbit finished, looking into the eyes of each and every member of the group sitting on the ground before him like pert plum puddings, their mouths agape. Things were going well in the Warren. They were quickly rebuilding the collapsed burrows and the new way of organising made every creature feel part of something. The rabbits had choice now and certainly did not need the President to tell them what to do.

The President was unhappy that the Chair-rabbit had not put his pawprint on the agreement and encouraged other leaders to do the same. This undermined his dream of a Field free from fighting; a Field where all creatures were rewarded for the effort they put into doing things. This was, the President believed, the shared dream of every creature whose leader had left a pawprint next to his on the agreement high in the branches of the cedar tree.

Not long after the Chair-rabbit's meeting with the most important group, the President heard rumours that the

Warren was offering the areas it swapped with more things in return for less. He knew the Chair-rabbit was trying to win favour, encouraging the creatures in these areas to think that the Warren was wonderful and making them wish they had a leader like him. In doing this, these creatures saw how all the rabbits were involved in making decisions, treated one another the same and each got the same amount of things collected and made by all the Warren's creatures. The same way the Chair-rabbit thought he had done, the President believed the Warren was taking away creatures' choices, forcing them to become more like the rabbits. He thought that the Chair-rabbit was catching these areas in a swapping trap, where they would do as he said out of fear that the Warren would stop swapping things they needed and loved with them.

The President was also scared. What if more creatures wanted to become like the Warren and it became the Field's most important area? What if the creatures of the Rise wanted to be like the Warren too, replacing him with lots of groups that had long meetings to discuss recommendations that they would pass on to another group to debate, and another and another after that before a decision was made? This thought was unbearable. The President believed the Rise's success was down to the way it organised itself and the opportunity it gave every creature to be rewarded for collecting and making more things: this was the vision of the dozen weasels all those seasons before and all the wanderers who had arrived since. If the Chair-rabbit had his way, this would all change and the Rise would no longer be the haven of opportunity for creatures in seasons to come.

The President needed a way for the Rise to become more powerful than the Warren.

After wracking his brain for many days and nights, fighting seemed the obvious choice. Many creatures still owed the Rise lots of things and the President knew he could use this to make other leaders join in fighting the Warren. With an army that big, they would certainly win. Although the Chair-rabbit thought everything was going well in the Warren, the rabbits were still very disorganised as they slowly adjusted to the new way of organising themselves and making decisions. But the President did not believe fighting was the answer. Most leaders had put their pawprints on the agreement to stop fighting in the Field once and for all. Too many creatures had already died and there was no need for more precious blood to be spilt. There had to be another way to scare the Warren, another way to make sure the Chair-rabbit never approached those leaders who had sided with the President and added their pawprints to the agreement.

One warm morning, as he ambled along a branch in his cedar, the sun's rays tickling each hair on his slender back, causing them to hum a sweet tune in delight, the answer came to him. The Rise had been in possession of the very thing to solve this problem for a long while – there was even a group of creatures dedicated to looking after it, just in case it ever needed to be used. This was a frightening thing about which those creatures who knew of its existence never spoke.

3

THE TONGUES

31

Being at the highest point in the Field, the Rise faced the worst of the storms that swept in over the Bottom Corner. Of all the areas of the Field, it was here that the thunder boomed loudest, the wind lashed most viciously, the rain fell in the thickest torrents and the lightning cracked the closest, threatening to shatter the fragile sky above. Lightning struck other parts of the Field too, like the Great Elm and the oaks in the Copse, which had spindly tops the vicious bolts were most attracted to. While it did not disturb the badgers, snug in their Sett away from the storm, it was a nuisance to the grey squirrels, sometimes splitting oak trunks in two, ruining their hollows, even killing grey squirrels curled up in their beds, hiding from the storm. The lightning storms usually came with thick sheets of rain, which gushed down the sides of the Rise into the Stream and Brook, and then into the River.

One particularly horrible, stormy afternoon during the fighting was different. Many of the Field's younger creatures had never seen a storm like it before. It had all the things a storm usually had: the wind whipped and whirled like a field mouse soldier's lash in the Copse all those seasons before. The dark clouds towered over the Field like a disapproving mother badger scolding her naughty cubs. The lightning snapped and cracked through the clouds like paws quickly reaching down to snatch a tree from the Field. This storm was missing one thing, though: the lashing rain which bit viciously into the hard ground like hungry little teeth. As the day wore on, the storm's intensity grew. Eventually, a particularly violent bolt of lightning, which threatened to split the sky in two, grabbed the top of a lonely, old chestnut tree on the top of the Rise and tore it into hundreds of splinters. Vicious, orange tongues suddenly appeared from nowhere and wrapped themselves around the splinters as they fell to the dry ground, where they continued to lick with no rain to arrest their enthusiasm. Many creatures had heard about these strange, greedy tongues that swallowed all they came in touch with, but none had seen them.

The only creatures living in this part of the Rise were two shrew brothers who, tucked away in their burrow, had heard the almighty crack as the lightning struck the old chestnut tree. Soon after, they had smelt the acrid, grey fog the tongues spat out as they swallowed all in their path. Wondering what the smell could be, they had poked their heads out to see.

The brothers had fled the Backwater when the fighting had broken out, making their way as quickly as they could to the Rise. They were very clever and had spent their days and nights in the Backwater thinking of ways swords could be lighter and sharper and canoes faster and easier to paddle.

The Chancellor had liked the brothers, making sure many of their ideas were used by the army so the Backwater had an advantage if fighting ever broke out. Soon the excitement of the Chancellor's favour wore off. They had been standing on the bank of the Backwater when he had told the shrews of his grand dream, making each of them feel they were chosen to do something important.

When they were young shrews, fresh out of the nest, the brothers had travelled the Field, exploring different areas and meeting many interesting creatures. On these travels, the brothers had learnt of the weird and wonderful things the other creatures did, said and wanted, all of which made them different than the shrews. The brothers had seen field mice try and make the Copse and the grey squirrels their own. They had seen the swapping almost ruin the Bottom Corner, the moles digging greedily to find as many glinting stones as they could. And they had seen creatures leave their homes and wander the Field to find another area where they could be safe, have food and be happy.

The brothers had known the Chancellor's dream was nothing new; it had been dreamed by many creatures before him. The same dream, at different moments by different creatures, but the same dream nonetheless. They had not wanted to be a part of this dream; they liked thinking of new and interesting ways of doing things that made the Field a better place, not a worse one. They had also had a new idea based on something they had never seen, but of which there were many old stories – stories of licking orange tongues and a grey fog that hung low over the ground, stinging eyes and making it difficult to breath. Stories of something far hotter than a large dark river stone warmed all day by the midsummer sun. And stories of something brighter than the crack of a lightning bolt as it lit up the Field for a split moment during a big storm.

Imagine, the brothers had thought, imagine if, when the tongues happened – however they did, for no creature knew for sure – they could be collected as little tongues and stored, like a red squirrel stored a hazelnut for a scrummy supper in a season or two? Imagine if, like a baby creature, these little tongues could be fed things and they grew into bigger tongues? And imagine what these big tongues could be used for? The brothers had not known; no creature did. There was one thing the brothers had felt certain about, though. If the tongues got big enough, they might be able to eat anything. Not just leaves, twigs and bits of fluff, but bigger things: nests, bushes, parched meadows, hedgerows and trees. They might even eat creatures – maybe even lots of creatures. If the hungry tongues were big enough, the brothers had mused, they might be able to eat anything.

If the tongues could be controlled, though, and only ate what they were given, imagine what they could be used for? If they were as bright as the old stories said, maybe they could turn the inky night into day? Creatures could then continue collecting and making things, dancing and singing long after the sun slipped over the horizon. If the rumours of their warmth were true, imagine all the things they could do? On their travels the brothers had seen the way the otters' fish dried quicker in the baking summer sun. Maybe they could be used to dry fish as quickly in winter as it did in summer? The brothers had also seen the grey squirrels shiver their way through the winter after the field mice had taken all the silky pods, leaving them with nothing to weave into jackets. Maybe the tongues could keep creatures snug and warm so they would never need silky pods or warm jackets to get through chilly winters again? The brothers had sat alongside field mice families in the Hedgerow after they had run out of silky cloth to swap and were forced to eat nuts stored in the Warren for many seasons. Mouldy and rotten, these were all they had. Nuts always tasted better when they were dry and warmed by the sun. Maybe the tongues could warm old nuts, making them yummier? This might mean less food went to waste, creatures able to sleep far happier with tummies full of food saved from ruin. And the brothers had seen snows melt happily into water that trickled across the Field, giving life to all plants and creatures on its gentle way through the Stream, Brook and Backwater to the River. Imagine if other things also melted when they got warm, like the golden nuggets the shrews collected? They might be melted to make tall things, round things and things with no shape at all.

So much might be possible if the brothers were able to find the illusive tongues and keep them alive to be used whenever a creature wanted. If this happened, the tongues could change the Field forever.

While many creatures before them, and likely after, thought that they were chosen to take control and lead the Field to something better, the brothers had seen things differently. They did not see change as controlling other creatures and making them do what they wanted. They did not see themselves as chosen, acting by the gift of a god to lead other creatures. They were just two ordinary shrews with a good idea. Not an idea to change who ruled who or how much one creature gave to another, but a change far bigger; a change not requiring an army or fighting or creatures being forced to do things by other creatures.

Up until then, change in the Field had come from two things. Creatures needed to be important, like the Queen or Chancellor, and have big armies and lots of creatures to collect and make what they told them to. Or creatures needed to band together, like the field mice who had gathered in front of the Queen's palace, shouting for things to change. But now just two creatures had found a way that could change the Field forever. The brothers had found something special, something which took the ability to change things out of the paws of the important and the many, and put it into the paws of ordinary creatures whose good ideas every creature could use.

Still, there were many unknowns and they had been unable to forget the dangers. What would happen if they found the tongues but could not control them? What if the tongues fell into the paws of the wrong creatures? Either of these things would be devastating. Given these uncertainties, the brothers had tried to keep their idea secret while they thought more about how it might work. Naturally, they had been excited, though, and wanted to tell their family and friends, who were excited too and wanted to tell theirs. Eventually, the Chancellor had heard about the idea and, just like the brothers, he had let his imagination run free. The tongues might wipe out armies and destroy areas which stood in the way of his grand dream coming true. What possibilities! The Chancellor had been excited and went to see the brothers to find out more. 'Is it really possible? Where do they come from? How long until I can have them?' Questions poured from his mouth like water gushing from the Brook into the Backwater after an autumn thunderstorm.

The Chancellor did not like the answers the brothers gave him. Hearing the idea was only based on stories and that the brothers had never actually seen the tongues themselves, he had been furious. 'What will it take?' he had asked. 'What needs to be done?'

'Firstly,' the brothers had replied, 'we need to find out if the stories about the tongues are true and, if they are, where they might be found.' This had made the Chancellor angrier. He stood in front of the brothers quivering with fury. His generals stood behind shaking their heads slowly in disdain like an oak tree's limbs moving in the breeze.

'How long will it take?' he had impatiently questioned again.

Looking down at their paws shuffling in the dust the brothers answered, 'We don't know, it could be never. It's just an idea.'

'It must be possible!' the Chancellor had yelled, flecks of spittle flying from his slender snout like angry bees from a hive. 'And you will do it!' He had paused and the brothers had shaken with fear. 'Otherwise you will be sent underground with all the other creatures who do not belong in the Backwater. The only creatures who belong here are shrews who want to become the most important creatures in the Field!' He had whirled around dramatically and left to return to his palace. His generals had followed closely like ants scurrying back to their nest. The first few drops of a rainstorm had begun to fall.

The brothers had been scared. What had they done? It was only an idea; they did not even know where to find the tongues, let alone how to keep them alive or grow them. No creature was meant to know about the idea yet, not least the Chancellor; he was the very last creature in the Field they had thought should know. The brothers' lives, and those of many other creatures, were now in danger. There was only one thing to do: they had to leave. The Backwater was no longer safe.

That night, as the shrews had lain snug in their beds whiffling gently, the brothers had crept from their burrow towards the edge of the Backwater. There was only one place they had thought they and their idea would be safe. It was a place the brothers had heard many things about but never visited. Like many creatures before them, the Rise had been their hope for safety and freedom. With one final look about to see if they were being followed, the brothers had left the Backwater and hurried across the Field towards the Rise before the Chancellor found out they were missing and sent soldiers to search for them.

Through the night's endless black curtains, they had pushed. Through the dawn too, the sun greeting them, grinning from ear to ear as it rejoiced in the new morning. Through the day, before the sun had given a cheeky wink and pulled another silky curtain of darkness across the sky behind it, the brothers had hurried. Finally, before dawn the next morning, the brothers had arrived at the Rise, their bodies aching and their paws wet and numb from the heavy dew and endless pounding. Their eyelids had hung low with tiredness. But finally, they and their idea had been safe, and maybe all the other creatures in the Field would be safe too.

32

Like all newcomers to the Rise, the brothers had been welcomed with outstretched paws. A mole, who had heard their paws thudding gently on the ground above her burrow, had poked out her nose to see what it could be. How tired and hungry the poor brothers had looked after their journey! Beckoning them eagerly into her family's home, she had given them food to lift their spirits and somewhere to lay their weary heads. Thanking the mole family, the next day the brothers had set out to find a spot for a new burrow of their own. While they missed the comforting, trickling dampness of the Backwater, they had been glad to be far away, safe from the Chancellor and his crazy dream.

The brothers liked being by themselves; it gave them space to think about their ideas without being interrupted by other nosy creatures. All over the Rise they had wandered, looking for the perfect spot, and before long, they had found it: a loamy bank on the edge of a small pond by a lonely, old chestnut tree. The soil was sweet and easy to dig, and nearby there was a pond of cool water with interesting things growing in it, making it feel a little like the Backwater. The old chestnut offered food and shelter from the sun, wind and rain. It was perfect. The brothers had started digging. Like all creatures in the Field, a natural home-making instinct kicked in without much thought having to be given, and before long the burrow was finished and they were living happily, far away from the Rise's other creatures.

The brothers had a few happy seasons in their new burrow before the Rise joined the fighting after the shrews' raid on the sled bound for the Hedgerow. Although they had not been in the Rise long, they had quickly become known for their wonderful ideas. Shortly after joining the fighting, the President had heard of the brothers from one of his generals and had asked to meet them. Obediently, the two brothers had traipsed across the Rise to the cedar tree. Sitting in his favourite spot on a branch far above the palace in the top of the tree, the President had asked for their help. 'We need to find something to make us better at fighting than the Backwater,' the President had begun in his calm voice. 'If our soldiers could have better swords, shields, spears and clubs than the Backwater's, we might win the fighting quicker, saving the lives of lots of creatures.' The President had finished, clasping his forepaws on his belly as he had lain back on the branch and gently clicked his claws in thought, the sun stroking his whiskers.

The brothers had had mixed feelings. On one paw, they could play an important part helping the Rise stop the fighting, but on the other, they were going to be fighting against their old home and some of their ideas might be used against their fellow shrews. It had been a difficult decision for the brothers and they had been torn. Knowing how dangerous the Chancellor and his ideas were, they had both felt the sooner the fighting stopped the better, for all creatures, and wanted to make this happen. So, they had done as the President asked, hiding away in their burrow to come up with many new ideas, only stopping for food and sleep. It had not taken them long to think of some clever new ideas for weapons and ways to make the Rise's army better than the Backwater's. When they had presented their ideas to the President and his generals every quarter moon, he had always become very excited and chose the best of them for the army to use.

33

The wind had whipped and the thunder had boomed across the sky. The orange tongues had licked the splinters of old chestnut tree as they fell silently to the ground, some as big as one of the shrews' canoes, some as small as a mole's digging claw. The brothers had looked at one another nervously as they poked their heads out of the burrow to have a look. What they had seen surprised them: there were the orange tongues, the thing they had thought about for so long without knowing if they were real. Braving the terrible wind, which threatened to pick them up and carry them away, the brothers had rushed to the remains of the chestnut tree for a closer look.

The old stories were true: the tongues were almost as bright as the sun and far too warm to pick up. Looking closer, the brothers had noticed that they had a ferocious hunger too. If they wanted to keep them like some creatures kept pet beetles and ants, they would need to be fed to stay alive. Luckily, the tongues enjoyed eating the dry chestnut splinters, of which there were lots underneath the old chestnut tree, and the brothers had frantically run backwards and forwards, building a pile of wood for doing just this.

Standing back, the brothers had watched the tongues devour the dry sticks they occasionally fed them and noticed that they kept trying to escape. Slowly the tongues had slurped along the grass, leaving nothing but a black, dusty mark. The brothers had also noticed that they did not like eating the little pebbles scattered in the grass. Maybe, they had thought, if the tongues did not like these, perhaps bigger ones could be used to stop them from escaping and eating other things. Once again, the brothers had rushed backwards and forwards collecting stones from the edge of the pond nearby, building a ring around the tongues to stop them sneaking away. They had then stood back once more with their forepaws crossed. They had done all they needed. The tongues had greedily licked away at the dry sticks and bark fed to them every now and again, unhappy to eat the pebbles and escape.

At last, the brothers had the thing that they had been thinking about for so long; the thing that had made them flee their home. Now that they had control of this thing, just like the Chancellor had done a few seasons before, the brothers had let their imaginations runs free, thinking of all the incredible things that they could do with them. They knew they had to be careful; having learnt their lesson in the Backwater, they had kept their secret to themselves while they mulled over who they should tell and why. Night after night they had stood by the tongues, feeding them the driest chestnut wood and discussing who should know about them and why. And night after night, as the tongues spat and crackled contentedly, sending showers of small orange fireflies into the night sky, the brothers had found no answer. After many moons of this, news of a particularly bloody battle between the Rise and Backwater's armies made its way to them and they had decided to tell the President – it might help to end the fighting once and for all.

Meeting the President and explaining how they had caught the tongues and kept them alive, he had immediately known the significance of what the brothers had done. Like all creatures in the Field, he had grown up hearing stories about the tongues and, like the other creatures, was unsure whether they were real. Needing to see them for himself, the President, followed by a few of his most loyal generals and the brothers, had left his cedar and rushed towards the old chestnut tree. He could not believe his eyes when he arrived. In the ring of stones were the tongues, happily licking the dry wood the brothers piled on.

What a wonderful thing they were, casting a friendly glow and radiating a warmth that tickled the President's paws as he waved them near. But what now? What could they be used for? Sitting in a circle with the President in the middle, the brothers had explained the many things that they thought the tongues might be able to do, like making bad food good and warming creatures in a chilly winter. They had also told of the bad things too, explaining their experiments to find out what the tongues liked to eat. The President and generals had been startled; apart from stones, the tongues had quickly devoured everything the brothers had fed them.

There had been a long silence and each creature in the circle had looked down at their paws with a worried expression. The President had spoken first. 'The creature who has control of the tongues can let them go free and they will eat everything standing in their way…?' His voice had tailed off; it was a scary thought. The circle had remained silent, pondering the mysterious thing licking away before them. Simply having the tongues would fill the Field's other creatures with fear, completely changing the way they acted towards the Rise. 'They could be the most important thing ever in the Field,' the President had mused quietly, his eyes staring wistfully into the tongues' warm glow. The brothers and generals had nodded gently but kept silent.

The President and generals had hurried back to the cedar tree, for they had many things to be getting on with, including thinking about how to use the tongues, or even whether they should. To help the brothers feed and guard them from creatures who might take them for themselves, the President had dispatched a group of soldiers to the old chestnut tree to lend a paw.

Although the Rise now had the tongues, the fighting kept on the same as before. Just as many creatures were given swords and spears and sent far away from their homes to fight for something they did not really know about, not fully understanding their significance, the soldiers guarding the tongues had stood by attentively, feeding them day and night. Such were the tongues' ferocious appetites, the chestnut wood soon ran out and the President then had to assign a general to organise a team to collect wood from other parts of the Rise and take it to them.

With the soldiers helping to keep the tongues alive, the brothers had spent long days testing their ideas. What happened if they tried to feed them this type of rock? What happened if they both huffed and puffed into the tongues? From all this testing, and the many days and nights they spent with them, the brothers had learnt that the tongues could not stand the wind and rain. One stormy evening, the rain had lashed the tongues, dampening the wood and making them shrink smaller and smaller. The brothers and soldiers had almost lost them. Only by sheltering them in the entrance of the brother's burrow, away from the soaking rain and wind like an endless breath from an enormous panting creature high in the sky had they been saved. When the President found out, he ordered a special fence and roof be built around the tongues to protect them. To let the stinging grey fog the tongues breathed when they ate escape, a neat hole was cut in the roof.

Not long after, the fighting had finally ended and any thought he may have needed to use the tongues against the Backwater disappeared from the President's mind. While all the soldiers in the Field celebrated the fighting's end, relieved to be returning home to their families, the brothers had continued their testing on the tongues. Beyond fighting, there were still many wonderful things that they might be used for.

The tongues were temperamental things, spitting when fed anything they did not like and difficult to handle, the fog stinging the brothers' eyes when they got too close. Nonetheless, the brothers had toiled away, hoping to find ways the tongues could be useful.

34

J ust after the big meeting at the Rise, and the President's morning walk when he remembered that he might have something to help solve his problem with the Warren, some rabbits travelling to the Rise heard a rumour about the tongues. Having grown up hearing stories about them, these rabbits knew the significance of the rumour if it was true. These travellers were not just visiting the Rise to learn about life there and meet new creatures, though, they were spies, sent by the Chair-rabbit to learn about the President's plans and what he thought about the Warren. Unlike many areas still only home to mostly one type of creature, like the Meadow, where still only hedgehogs lived, being home to lots of different creatures made it easy for the spies to blend in on the Rise. Learning a little of the language the creatures of the Rise spoke, the spies listened carefully for gossip, finding out lots of interesting things. Asking a little question here and there, eavesdropping on creatures sitting outside their burrows chatting to one another in the evening as the sun went down, the spies gradually learnt that the tongues were being kept in a far corner of the Rise with two score of soldiers guarding them.

One inky night, with the clouds hiding the moon like droopy eyelids refusing to open in their sleep, the spies crept towards the old chestnut tree to see the tongues for themselves. A little way off, they stopped suddenly and huddled behind a bramble bush, peering towards the tree. It was unmistakeable. Through the gloom, the spies saw the tongues' orange glow between gaps in the new fence, illuminating the soldiers guarding them. And heavily guarded it was too, the fierce soldiers armed with the finest swords and spears scowling in the shadows. Unable to do anything against this guard, the spies returned to their burrow to hatch a plan.

A few days later, half a score of soldiers journeyed over the Rise to relieve some of their compatriots guarding the tongues. Hiding behind the same bramble bush as before, the rabbit spies waited patiently for the soldiers and then sprung out unexpectedly, wrestling them to the ground. With a few blows from the swords and spears the soldiers had been carrying only moments earlier, the spies brutally killed them. Taking their bright jackets and weapons, they continued on to the old chestnut tree in disguise. The spies had spent the last few days and nights hiding in this bramble bush beside the path watching the soldiers go back and forth, learning how tired soldiers were replaced. Sometimes only a few were left guarding the tongues before new ones arrived.

Dressed and armed like soldiers from the Rise, the other soldiers took little notice of the spies beyond a gentle nod or wink when they arrived at the old chestnut tree. Taking up positions where they were told, the spies stood against the fence, the tongues warming their backs in the autumn evening chill. As it got dark, the soldiers broke to rest their paws and have a little food to keep them going through the long night. While eating pawfuls of berries and nuts and drinking water in a wooden pitcher from the nearby pond, one of the spies quickly sneaked a couple of drops from a tiny stone vial into the water vessel. The juice of a fungus that grew far underground in the Warren, the drops had been used by the rabbits for as long as they could remember. A big dose could easily kill an enemy, while a middle dose put a guard to sleep, and a little dose was said to be the best cure for the common rabbit cold. It was not long before the soldiers from the Rise were slumped at their posts, slipping to the ground and curling into sleeping balls, their snores gently shaking the earth under the spies' paws like a marching army approaching from a long way off. The shrew brothers, who often supped with the soldiers, were snoring too, just inside the entrance to their burrow where they had been discussing a new idea for something or other and drawing a picture in the dust with a stubby stick.

Now was the spies' chance. One by one, they each picked up one of the long sticks that lay in a neat pile next to the fence around the tongues, which were as tall as them and wrapped in dry grass and flakes of birch bark. Rarely used, these sticks were kept at the ready, just in case the tongues needed to be quickly moved to escape wind, rain or an attack. The tongues liked the grass and dry bark and were soon greedily licking one of the sticks held by the spies. The spies did not have long; each of them could only carry one stick and the tongues devoured them quickly. It would also not be long before the soldiers awoke and saw some of the sticks and the rabbit soldiers gone. Upon hearing this, the President would immediately be suspicious...

The spies left the snoring soldiers and hurried away towards to the Warren. Approaching the edge of the Rise, they dared not slow down, only stopping briefly when the tongues ate too much of one stick and they had to let them greedily start on another. Throughout the night the spies ran, occasionally looking behind to see if they were being followed. The tongues shone brightly through the thick darkness of the moonless gloom. As the sun rose shyly behind heavy clouds, the spies kept on as fast as they could, their paws aching as they pounded the hard ground again and again. They kept running, the sound of their drumming feet, thumping hearts and gasping breaths filling their ears, numbing all other senses. In the middle of the next night, the spies finally arrived exhausted in the Warren. The tongues were eating through the end of the last stick and spluttered angrily with hunger.

To keep their secret, the spies had not sent a messenger to the Warren to tell the Chair-rabbit what they had found. With no arrival party to greet them, the spies halted suddenly at an entrance guarded by scowling rabbit soldiers with heavy wooden clubs. Chests heaving, they gasped who they were and what they were doing. One of the spies quickly snatched the closest soldier's club and thrust its end against the spluttering tongues. Being neither dried grass nor bark, the tongues took a little longer to decide whether they liked the hard wood, but soon they did and started to lick the club hungrily – and not a moment too soon; the tongues ran out of stick to eat, coughed once or twice and then disappeared into thin air.

Half the spies stayed at the entrance to guard the tongues while the rest rushed to the biggest burrow where the most important group were gathered. Once the home of the disgraced Tsar and his family, this burrow was spectacularly decorated, its ceiling so high it did not seem that there was one. Shimmery fabrics stolen from the Hedgerow when the rabbits had had their first uprising lined the walls and covered the floor. In the middle of the burrow the members of the most important group sat in a circle around the Chair-rabbit. The spies burst in, panting heavily. Startled, the Chair-rabbit took a moment to recognise them before jumping up and rushing over – he had eagerly awaited their return. Before beckoning them sit and rest their exhausted limbs, the Chair-rabbit hurriedly asked what they had discovered from the Rise. The spies dutifully told him about the thing they had just risked life and paw to bring back to their home.

The Chair-rabbit could not believe it. The tongues were real? Not just a story every creature in the Field knew about? As the spies told the story, he became confused. Had they simply just found out that the Rise had the tongues? Tears of defeat filled the Chair-rabbit's eyes and he buried his face in his paws as the spies continued, telling the story of how they'd disguised themselves as soldiers and sent the guards to sleep, stealing some of the tongues and dashing home back over the Field. The Chair-rabbit's paws slowly rose from his felty cheeks, his tears turning from those of despair to those of happiness. Higher his paws rose still, until they could go no further and he shook them with triumph. The Rise had the tongues, but now the Warren had them too! He had heard stories about the things the tongues could do. If they really did all the old stories said, the Warren would be just as strong as the Rise. And, if they were the only two areas which had them, the two of them would now be more important than all the other areas in the Field.

After he had seen the tongues for himself, admiring their warmth, brightness and how quickly they devoured the wood they were fed, the Chair-rabbit ordered digging to start immediately on a special burrow for them to live in. This burrow would have small tunnels going straight up to the meadow above so the tongues had lots of fresh air to keep them healthy and so the grey, stinging fog had somewhere to escape. After this, the Chair-rabbit returned to a small burrow just off the biggest one. Laying down, he drew a thick, red silky blanket over himself snuggly. In ordering the digging of this burrow, he had bypassed all the groups which made decisions.

Laying there, giddy with glee and unable to sleep, the Chair-rabbit could not believe the Warren's luck. He let his mind drift; there must be something or some creature somewhere helping the Warren. He could think of no other reason why its fortunes had changed so quickly. It now had a completely different way of organising itself and making decisions, a big army and the tongues. Snuggling deeper into the blanket, it struck him like the bolt of lightning that had brought the tongues to the Field: he had just become one of the most important creatures ever in the Field. He could barely believe it; he had been an ordinary rabbit most of his life, doing whatever all the other rabbits did when the field mice told them to. His family had never known any important rabbits, like those who were friends of the Tsar or who helped make decisions. Look what he had become, he thought, there must be a god.

The Field was changing quickly. Now ordinary creatures, not just kings, queens, tsars, tsarinas, emperors, empresses, princes, princesses, chiefs, chieftesses, priests, priestesses, rajahs and ranis could make decisions and have the opportunity to change the Field, perhaps forever. The shrew brothers' ideas to help in the fighting and their discovery of the tongues meant that they had changed the Field. While not many creatures knew of them, particularly outside the Rise, they were important creatures. It was the same for the Chair-rabbit, and all the other rabbits who were part of the groups which made decisions; their ideas were important.

35

As dawn broke the morning following the spies'
escape, the soldiers guarding the tongues awoke
and sat dazed, wondering what had happened to
them. Heads clearing, they slowly helped one another up
and pieced together the events of the previous evening.
They remembered eating pawfuls of berries and nuts, and
some rabbit soldiers they had never seen before, then they
remembered nothing. Surveying each other suspiciously,
they noticed the faces of the rabbit soldiers had gone –
something was not right. Looking around the stone circle,
they noticed many of the sticks to carry the tongues in an
emergency were missing. One of the soldiers, whose head
pounded the least, for he had taken the smallest slurp of
the fungi-juice-laced water, ran quickly to the cedar tree to
explain to the President what had happened.

The soldiers were embarrassed. What had they done?
Who were the rabbits and where were they from? Was it just
the generals and the President testing how well they guarded
the tongues? Or had some other creatures in the Field stolen

the tongues for themselves? If so, had they been caught before they left the Rise? With many unanswered questions; their hearts hung heavy with guilt.

Upon hearing the news, the President thought the worst, pacing backwards and forwards along his favourite cedar branch deep in thought, pondering what to do next. Not long after, his fears were confirmed. A general arrived, telling him that soldiers keeping watch during the night where the Rise met the lush meadow had seen a bright orange glow leave the Rise and head towards the Warren. The tongues were a closely guarded secret and these soldiers had not known what the orange glow meant. Scared of something so strange, they had not bothered to follow or look more closely to find out what it was.

The President could not be angry. When the shrew brothers had first told him of the tongues, he had known something bad might happen; that having something like this would change how other creatures in the Field acted towards the Rise – both the friendly, like the Hedgerow, and the less so, like the Warren. He had known that, when other creatures learnt of the tongues, they would want them. Now it had happened: two areas with different views on organising and making decisions had the tongues. Did the Chair-rabbit of the Warren know what they could do; the damage they could inflict? The President, his generals and the shrew brothers did not fully know for themselves. Now they had to find out.

The President immediately sent for the brothers and, when they arrived, told them in low tones what had happened. The brothers hung their heads and shuffled their feet awkwardly as they listened, scared of what they had unleashed. A friendly creature, the President patted the brothers on their backs to reassure them that it was not their fault. It did no good. The brothers remained downcast, not daring to raise their eyes to meet his. The President smiled warmly, like a father dormouse whose pup had just accidently dropped a berry in the dust, before telling the brothers of his plan. 'We must do lots of testing to find out what the tongues can really do.' He paused and the brothers slowly raised their heads to meet his gaze. 'This will not only help us understand what we can do if we ever want to use them, but also what others can do…' He stopped, his head nodding gently, and a few long moments passed before he added, '…Can do, to us.'

That same morning, the Chair-rabbit called a meeting of the most important group. Seated on the colourful, silky cloth-clad floor in the biggest burrow, he excitedly told the group about the tongues, just like a young bunny might tell a friend about a new toy their father had carved them. The rabbits in the group, old, young and everything in between, chattered excitedly – what an amazing thing for the Warren to have! Banging his paws on the floor in anger at the interruption, the Chair-rabbit brought the burrow back to silence before continuing, 'I am thinking that another group must be being made to explore what the tongues can be doing.' The members nodded in agreement; it was very important that they knew what they were dealing with. He added, 'And myself, I am putting forward to be the very Chair-rabbit of this group too.' They agreed again, some even waving their paws in the air like reeds in a stiff breeze along the edge of the Backwater, hoping to be picked for the group – it sounded far more exciting than being part of the groups that discussed how many entrances the Warren needed or which tunnels should be lengthened and which abandoned completely. Hastily picking a few of the waving paws, the Chair-rabbit immediately ended the meeting and the rest of the members filed out of the big burrow so a meeting of the new group for the tongues could start. Just as the President had done, this new group decided more testing was needed to find out what the tongues could do, how the Warren could use them and what the Rise could use them for too.

36

The President and Chair-rabbit both assigned many creatures to help find out what the tongues could do. Lots of different things were fed to them to see what would happen. On the ground above the Warren, and in parts of the Rise where no creatures lived, the tongues were set free to see how they would respond. These tests told both leaders all they needed to know: the tongues had an insatiable hunger. Set free to eat whatever they wanted, they were truly devastating, not slowing if a nest, tree or even a creature got in their way. Once free, only two things stopped them: running out of something to eat or a big rainstorm. Starving the tongues or drowning them slowly with heavy, paw-sized raindrops, which made them pop and hiss in complaint, were the only ways to make the tongues disappear.

While the testing was happening, the President and Chair-rabbit continued with their plans to make the Field more like they thought it should be. The President put much effort into forming the three groups agreed at the meeting in the Rise. In retort, the Chair-rabbit gathered around him leaders that, like him, were angered at the thought the President's new groups would make some of the Field's areas more like the Rise, in turn making it more important.

It was not long before the three big groups with representatives from many areas started holding their meetings in the Brush with many important things discussed. Things like, how all the areas should get along with one another and how arguments between areas could be resolved without fighting. The group in charge of making rules set about debating those that they thought the areas of the Rise should allow. The group in charge of swapping changed all the agreements made during the fighting so it was easier for the creatures who still needed to swap things back with the Rise to do so. And the group in charge of rebuilding nests and burrows in areas destroyed by the fighting brought together builders, burrowers and advisors from areas with less damage to help. Travelling from one area to the next, these creatures weaved new nests, dug new burrows and gave creatures new ideas, such as different ways that they could choose a leader and become more involved in making decisions themselves.

With these new ideas set free in their imaginations like badger cubs freed from the Sett into the Meadow on the first day of spring, one by one, creatures in many areas across the Field had their own small uprisings, much as had happened in the Hedgerow and Warren. Gradually, these uprisings had success, a leader forced to stand aside and a vote cast to choose a new one. More often than not, this leader was little better than the last. When this happened, the creatures got bored and, realising things were no better than before, decided another new leader might change things. So, the whole thing was gone through all over again, often with the same outcome.

The Chair-rabbit was doing a similar thing, helping areas left worse off by the fighting rebuild and swapping things with them. This was often done for nothing if they promised to be closer friends with the Warren and told creatures from the areas supporting the Rise to go away if they ever came near. And, much like the President's group of builders, burrowers and advisors, those from the Warren told every creature in each area they helped of the wonderful way the Warren organised itself and made decisions. Many creatures liked the sound of this very much, just as many creatures were excited by the way Rise did things, and had their own uprisings, choosing a new chair-creature to lead them and forming lots of groups to decide how to get things done. Then the creatures continued on their merry way, full of hope things would be different and better. Different, they certainly were. Better? Many quickly realised not so.

37

Seeing each other's success spreading their ideas to different areas of the Field, the President and Chair-rabbit grew scared that these ideas would creep into the areas which had sided with them, and even their own areas too. Everything they believed in and had fought for could be taken away from them. Both knew that this was the thing the other feared the most.

Secrets never stayed so for long in the Field and the leaders of many areas friendly with the Rise became worried when they heard about the tongues. The Prime Minister of the Hedgerow, being neighbour to the Warren, felt uncomfortable that there was something so close which could eat it and all its creatures in the blink of a beady field mouse eye. The President tried to reassure the Prime Minister at one of the meetings of the three groups in the Brush, but he could not be calmed. 'It worries me having those awful tongue things so close to my Hedgerow!' He spoke hurriedly, his clasped paws shaking. 'I haven't dared tell any creature about it – not even the Queen knows. Gosh, what would she say?'

The President tried to reassure him again. 'We've had the tongues far longer than the Warren and we know how to use them better…' Patting the Prime Minister on the back the same way he had the shrew brothers some seasons before, he added, 'We will always look after the Hedgerow if something happens.' This was not enough for the Prime Minister; he believed the Hedgerow was still one of the Field's most important areas. How could the Hedgerow be important if other creatures could reduce it to a pile of grey dust in an instant?

Many field mice had moved to the Rise after the grey squirrels', rats' and rabbits' uprisings had thrown the Hedgerow into disarray and it had been unable to swap as much as before. Like most creatures who wandered to the Rise, these field mice sought a new beginning, distancing themselves from the things the Hedgerow had done in the past. Many words in the language of the Rise were shared with Field Mouse, and the way they spoke and many things they ate were similar too. The two areas had always been close friends, and they had grown closer when the Rise had sided with the Hedgerow during the fighting and the Prime Minister had supported the President's new groups at the big meeting at the Rise. While not as important as it once was, many of the Field's leaders still looked up to the Hedgerow, remembering how it had started the swapping they now all relied upon, and how it had once ruled almost half the Field. When they saw the Prime Minister supporting the Rise, they thought it would be a good idea too, and the President knew this.

When the Prime Minister arrived on a surprise visit to the Rise only a few moons after their encounter in the

Brush, the President knew why he had come. The Prime Minister reminded him of the two areas' friendship, many seasons old, and how they had always helped one another. The President nodded in agreement and the Prime Minister finished with a tear in his eye. 'I do not want you to have to look after all the creatures in the Field, including us in the Hedgerow, by yourselves; it is too much of a burden for one area. We want to help, but we need the tongues to do that.'

The President understood; if the Warren used the tongues against the Hedgerow, it might be too late for the Rise to help them. He also had an inkling that the Prime Minister was not explaining his main reason: he did not want to be beholden or indebted to the Rise. Things could change quickly in the Field and neither leader knew what would happen in seasons to come. The Rise could lose the tongues or a sickness could spread, like in the Warren all those seasons ago. Or simply, the two leaders might disagree on something or other and no longer be friendly. The President knew all these things and was also worried about the Warren. Many areas around it were starting to organise and make decisions just like they did. These areas no longer had sultans, empresses, kings or tsars, they now had chair-creatures that led important groups that made decisions on recommendations from groups below them and groups below those.

The opinions of the creatures of the Hedgerow and Rise differed on many things, but they did agree creatures should be rewarded for the effort they put into collecting and making things for themselves to swap with other creatures. This united them in their dislike for the way the Warren did things. They both thought their area did things best and that other areas should make decisions and organise themselves like they did, not the Warren.

Returning to the Hedgerow that evening after his meeting with the President, the Prime Minister was followed closely behind by a group of soldiers from the Rise surrounding a sled carrying a small circle of stones. In the middle of these stones lay the tongues, hungrily licking the wood the soldiers fed them every now and again. Strutting proudly in front, the Prime Minister's smile ran from one velvety, round ear to the other. The Hedgerow now had the tongues and, once again, they were one of the Field's most important areas.

Just like the Rise and Warren, when the Hedgerow got the tongues, the Prime Minister ordered that lots of testing be done so that they had a better idea what they could do. With his spies everywhere, the Chair-rabbit was most unhappy when he found out. How could the Rise give something like the tongues to another area? Especially one like the Hedgerow which had invaded many areas in the past, including the Warren. Although there was no agreement between the Rise and Warren about the tongues, the Chair-rabbit felt that, by only the two of them having their warm, orange glow, an unspoken trust had formed between the two leaders. The President had broken this, not only by giving the tongues to another area, but by giving them to one so close to the Warren.

The Chair-rabbit was unusually upset and felt like revenge. Wrapped in his red, silky blanket, tossing, turning and trying to sleep, he whispered to himself, 'The President must be knowing what it is being like to have betrayal the way he has been doing; to be having these tongues belonging to creatures so close to him.'

38

A small area, the Pond was tucked between the far end of the Rise and the Beavers' Brook. With the Rise on one side and willows and brambles on the other, the Pond got little sunlight, making it a dark, dank place. Muddy and infested with insects which loved to bite, it was not the kind of spot many creatures wished to call home, except for the frogs. Taking life very seriously and smiling rarely, the frogs did not mind the damp, happy to slink into the murky water and bury themselves in the mud to escape the insects.

A horrid place to visit, few creatures from other areas ventured to the Pond so the Frogs kept to themselves, swapping little. While the spies who stole the tongues had been in the Rise, many other rabbits had travelled across the Field at the orders of the Chair-rabbit to find out things about other areas which might be useful to the Warren. Some of the spies had visited the Pond and, apart from finding it a truly harrowing experience (rabbits are not fond of damp, preferring to be snug and dry underground), they had discovered the old frog Emperor had recently died, leaving the Pond in disarray. The Emperor had controlled everything in day-to-day life in the Pond and was well loved but had no children. The frogs were finding it difficult to choose another creature to take over. To the spies, this had been interesting: the Pond was exactly the sort of place that would benefit from doing things like the Warren. On the other paw, it was next to the Rise and this would make the President angry.

The spies had gone straight back to the Warren and told the Chair-rabbit but, having just got the tongues, his mind was on other things and he had thought no more of it. The Pond was a long way from the Warren and the frogs were odd creatures, difficult to get along with.

The night after the Chair-rabbit discovered the Hedgerow had been given the tongues, he lay, tossing feverishly in his red, silky blanket. Wracking his brains for a way to get revenge, he recalled the stories the spies had told him about the strange Pond some moons before.

Once again, the Chair-rabbit called an urgent meeting of the most important group, where he proposed that some ambassadors must be sent there, much like the Queen had done for the Riverbank and Copse many seasons before. 'This grouping of ambassadors,' he proclaimed loudly to the group, 'will be going to these frogs and explaining that the President is being trying very, very hard to force changes to some areas in the way they are organising themselves and making their decisions so they are being more like the Rise.' He continued breathlessly, 'These frogs will be being told by these ambassadors, because they are being neighbours of the

Rise and oh-so-difficult finding it to be choosing a new frog to be the leader-frog, that they are in very much danger of having the Rise being starting to tell them how they are to be doing their own things. This is not so good. In the Rise it is being every creature for themselves. No creature is looking after another creature. They have long ago been losing the sense of living and doing things all together. We rabbits are knowing these things are being so, so important in the Field.'

The Chair-rabbit paused, looking around the big burrow into the eyes of each of the members sitting before him. They stared back unblinkingly, growing looks of puzzlement on their faces. 'It is making the most perfect of all sense,' the Chair-rabbit continued. 'These ambassadors will be kindly telling these frogs of the other way, of *our* way. They will be telling these frogs stories most wonderful of our struggle to be being free from that wicked Tsar. Of our perfected way of having groups up here and groups down there and groups all over the place to be making sure lots and lots and lots and lots of creatures are being able to be helping in the making of decisions! And of the way us creatures in the Warren are all being the same and having the things of the same amount we all are being collecting and making and swapping.' There was a murmur of agreement around the burrow, but the puzzled looks remained. 'These frogs will be most liking our ideas, as any creature who is being sensible is doing. We will be offering these frogs help to be choosing a new leader and to be building burrows that are being very new and where they can be living and meeting. And most finally, we will be offering these frogs to swap some weapons and some food to them in return for not so much.'

The Chair-rabbit finally stopped and drew breath, surveying the creatures before him in detail again. He enjoyed talking and stood beaming from the tip of one long, pointy ear to the other. The members looked at one another befuddled. Had he gone mad? The Warren had done similar things with other areas, but never like this and with such generosity. The Chair-rabbit enjoyed the moment. He felt the members were balanced in his paw in anticipation; they could feel there was more to the Chair-rabbit's plan. He turned his paw over and let them drop. 'I am proposing that these ambassadors are being offering all of these things to these frogs for them to be allowing us to have own incy-wincy part of their Pond where we can be having some space for digging one or two or three or seven burrows. In these burrows, our soldiers will be some of them living and giving defending help to the Pond from any creature who is being trying to attack them. By being there and all of them doing these things, these soldiers will be being very close to the Rise and keeping a very, very close beady eye on the President.'

The members sighed together, thinking that the Chair-rabbit had finished, but this was not all, he still had more to say. Some members felt like rolling their eyes but thought better of it. 'Just like it is being right here in the Warren, these little burrows in the Pond will be having a most special burrow, a sort of burrow where these tongues can some of them be being kept as very close to the Rise as they can possibly be without actually being on the Rise.' Now he paused for breath and dramatic effect. The mouths of the members before him fell open. 'Being this way, if ever the Rise or the Hedgerow are being choosing to use these tongues against us, we will be having no delay, we will be retaliating as straight away as we certainly, possibly can!'

As he finished, the bottom jaws of most of the members fell as far as they could. Of course, they were upset, like the Chair-rabbit, that the Rise had given the Hedgerow some of the tongues, but doing what he proposed would really upset the President. They knew the Rise had been friends with the Hedgerow for many seasons, and that the Hedgerow was responsible for the tongues given to them – the Prime Minister had not let the President have his own bit of the Hedgerow to keep them and his soldiers. The Chair-rabbit's plan was different.

There was a long silence broken only by the Chair-rabbit's paws as he excitedly shuffled from one to the other. Suddenly, many members of the group started shouting all at once. Some new to the group and desperate to make a good impression thought it was a great idea that the Warren was standing up to the Rise. Many older members were deeply unhappy; they knew this would upset the President and were scared what would happen.

Up until now, simply having the tongues had been enough to stop the Rise and Warren using them, not only on each other, but on other areas too. If the Rise chose to use them against an area friendly with the Warren, the Chair-rabbit would have to step in to stop it, and the same for the President if the Warren set them on a friend of the Rise. A strange situation had emerged. With a few of exceptions here and there, half the Field who were friendly with the Rise were fighting the other half who were friendly with the Warren. Yet there was no fighting. Each side knew using the tongues might mean they would be destroyed. It was a scary thought, and one which made each side very careful not to upset the other.

The Chair-rabbit sat quietly as the older members explained why they thought it was a bad idea. After a while, he grew bored of listening and stood up again. He was not happy. Organising themselves in the way they did was the very reason the Chair-rabbit was leader of the Warren, but it annoyed him that every decision had to be discussed by many groups and he did not get his own way. In recent seasons, he had started trying to make more decisions himself, ignoring the recommendations of all the other groups below the most important group, and even that one too. He liked getting his own way. When members of the important group disagreed with him, he often suggested to other members that the dissenters had been in the group too long or were not having good ideas and needed replacing, usually by creatures the Chair-rabbit recommended himself – creatures he knew would agree with him. Gradually, the most important group had filled with members who rarely questioned the Chair-rabbit's ideas, and he usually got what he wanted.

This situation was different. Not for a long while had so many members disagreed with him. He did not like it and explained his idea again, fearing many were only disagreeing because they did not understand. After the second explanation, many still disagreed with him and he lost his temper. Ranting and raving, the Chair-rabbit threatened every member, telling them that he would have them removed from the group and spread rumours about things he knew they had done. As often happened, they changed their minds and the Chair-rabbit got his own way. He grinned and bowed to them all in thanks before disappearing in a blink to his small burrow to rest.

Soon after, the rabbit ambassadors left the Warren, heading towards the Pond. Before long, they returned; it had been easy negotiating with the frogs. With no leader, or even a group of creatures to make decisions, the Pond was in chaos. The rabbit ambassadors seized the opportunity, speaking to many of the old Emperor's friends who were bickering and jostling, trying to become the new Emperor. Every one of these frogs thought differently about what should happen to the Pond, but all were scared when the ambassadors told them about what the President was doing across the Field – so scared, in fact, that they all happily agreed to help from the Warren to protect them.

The day after the ambassadors returned to the Warren, a few score soldiers and burrowers headed to the Pond to start digging burrows in the soggy soil. The Chair-rabbit's plan had worked and now the Warren's soldiers and the tongues had a new home close to the Rise.

39

Soldiers on lookout at the edge of the Rise saw all this toing and froing from the Warren to the Pond and the President was told. He had known the Chairrabbit would not be happy having the tongues so close in the Hedgerow and that something like this would happen. Not long after the President was told, lookouts reported that they had seen an orange glow, flickering and dancing like a butterfly across the Field in the dead of night. Arriving at the Pond, the glow had disappeared immediately and not been seen since. Being a practical creature, the President had a strong feeling that he knew what was happening, that, seeking revenge, the Chair-rabbit was doing to the Rise as he felt it had done to them, giving the tongues to its closest neighbour. How strange, the President thought, the frogs always kept to themselves, having little to do with other areas. To find out for certain, the President sent some spies to the Pond to investigate.

The answer came back quickly. Just as the spies from the Warren had found when they visited the Pond, the frogs happily blabbed about almost everything to any creature that would listen. This way, the President found out that the Chair-rabbit had not given the tongues to the Pond but promised to protect them from the Rise and help them choose a new leader in exchange for keeping a few of the Warren's soldiers and the tongues there. The President was angry; he believed his main role was as protector of the creatures in the Rise. Now the Warren had the tongues so close to them, he felt he had failed. Not only this, if the frogs chose to organise themselves like the rabbits, maybe the worst could happen, maybe the creatures in the Rise would see it and want to do it too. This would be the end of the special understanding that existed between the creatures of the Rise, as well as his presidency and everything he had spent so many seasons striving for.

In the President's eyes, there was only one thing to do: he had to solve the problem directly and talk to the Chair-rabbit. With relations between the two areas being so unfriendly, the President's advisors thought it unsafe for him to go to the Warren himself. Instead, a spritely young vole ambassador was sent in his place, who ran frantically between the two areas, taking the President's messages to the Chair-rabbit and back again.

To begin, the vole ambassador simply told the Chair-rabbit straight: 'The President knows you have soldiers in the Pond and are keeping some of the tongues there.'

The Chair-rabbit laughed heartily, denying it completely. 'How horrible is it being in the Pond?' the Chair-rabbit scoffed. 'There it is being the darkest and dampest of all places, it would be of interest for the reason being what?

Plus,' he added, 'I am not even beginning to know what are these tongue things that you are being telling me of.'

The ambassador rolled his eyes and hurried back to the Rise. There was nothing to gain arguing with the Chair-rabbit. Relaying this message, the President pinched his nose in thought and then sent the ambassador straight back to the Warren. 'Tell the Chair-rabbit I know more about what he is doing in the Pond. I know he is helping the frogs to organise themselves like the Warren. I know he is swapping weapons and food in return for nothing other than somewhere to have a few burrows for the tongues and soldiers to live.'

When the ambassador repeated this to the Chair-rabbit, he scoffed as before, denying it completely once again. 'I am knowing not where your President has been getting these ideas so crazy! Maybe... Maybe he is not okay? Maybe he is not being the fittest of presidents. Have you been ever thinking of that? Maybe should you be telling your friends and families of these things?' The Chair-rabbit chuckled to himself and bid the ambassador farewell from the biggest burrow in the Warren where he lay in the middle, reclined on a soft, silky rug, greener than the hedgehog's Meadow in early spring.

Similar messages went back and forth between the Rise and Warren over and over again, the exhausted ambassador spending many days traipsing between the two areas. With little progress, and the continued questioning of his soundness of mind by the Chair-rabbit, the President grew uneasy. Recently, spies had told him they had seen rabbits helping the frogs dig a new burrow in the Pond. This was not just any burrow; it was big enough for lots of creatures to meet and make recommendations to a group led by a recently chosen chair-frog. Up until now, although he had given the Hedgerow the tongues, neither the President nor the Chair-rabbit had encouraged an area so close to the other to change the way it organised itself to be more like theirs. Things had gone too far.

The ambassador went back to the Warren once again with a new message. 'The President says that you have four moons to remove your soldiers and the tongues from the Pond.' He trembled nervously, the tips of his ears shaking. 'If this does not happen, the President will order that the tongues be set loose on the Warren. If he does this, the Field will finally see what happens when the tongues are set free.'

The Chair-rabbit stared blankly. Until now, neither side had threatened to use the tongues. Knowing another area had them was enough. But the words tumbling from between the ambassador's chattering teeth were a real threat. Both leaders knew what it could mean: using the tongues might not just see the Warren or Hedgerow destroyed. If the tongues grew and grew and were hungry enough, maybe other areas would be as well.

Maybe all areas – the whole Field.

The Field in all its beauty, the only place the creatures knew existed. The place where many different creatures were born, breathed and died. The place where many things had happened, were happening and would happen. The place where winter froze the River and frosted the branches of the oaks in the Copse. The place where spring sunshine burst life from the ground and breezes sent waves chasing themselves through the grass of the meadows. The place where summer sun dried the meadow flowers, spilling the seeds forth onto the ground. And the place where autumn rains carried these seeds in bubbling streams to other parts of the Field, where they would lay patiently for the spring to wake them.

Each leader was proud and would not stand down, neither able to bear the thought of a Field where all the areas organised themselves and made decisions the same way as the other.

As the ambassador finished relaying the President's threat, the Chair-rabbit spat his answer contemptuously back. 'Your crazy president, you be telling him that if he be unleashing these tongues on the Warren it will most certainly be forcing us to be doing the same thing back to the Rise.' He paused to let his words sink in. 'It is being not only that, I will also be deciding to unleash our tongues on the areas who are being friendly with the Rise. The Hedgerow… The Riverbank…' He tailed off.

Hearing the ambassador's recount, the President knew nothing else could be done. He and the Chair-rabbit had to agree on something or their areas, and even the whole Field, might be destroyed. Neither wanted to concede first. The ambassador was sent back to the Warren once more. Exhausted from remembering all the different messages and running back and forth across the Field, the ambassador breathlessly delivered the President's response to the Chair-rabbit. 'Nothing has changed. Remove your soldiers and tongues from the Pond or the Rise will use the tongues against the Warren… And the Pond.' He curled his lip aggressively and narrowed his eyes, tilting his head slightly to the side as he added, 'Even if you choose to use the tongues against us.'

Like a young weasel tossing a spiky conker back to a playmate, the Chair-rabbit sent the ambassador back to the President. 'You be telling your President that it be not mattering that much, I will too most certainly be using these tongues against the Rise.' A smile crept across the Chair-rabbit's downy face as he said this. 'And also… You be telling your craziest of presidents that we have been now keeping these tongues in lots and lots and lots of areas all over the Field; they are not just being in the Pond. You are knowing what this is being meaning?' The ambassador shook his head slowly and the Chair-rabbit laughed. 'It is being meaning that we can be using these tongues better by far than your craziest president will be using them, that is what this is being meaning!'

The President knew this was not true. The Rise had spies in all areas and had neither seen nor heard anything to prove that the Warren had the tongues in any other area than the Pond. The Chair-rabbit was bluffing, trying to scare the President so he would admit defeat first.

The four moons were counting down.

40

Neither leader could sleep on the night of the last moon. Leaving their burrows, they both went out into the mild summer night. The sky was cloudless, the stars splayed across it far above them, twinkling like a pawful of the moles' shining stones. A long way apart, both the President and Chair-rabbit lay down on their backs and looked up at the same stars. A warm breeze tickled their ears, carrying the tingly, sweet scent of meadow flowers to their noses.

It was a special night – a night that made living through the Field's long, hard winter worthwhile. A night where a creature felt truly alive and part of something special as they heard others outside enjoying it the same as them. The two leaders shared the joy of this moment. The joy of being part of a Field where, although creatures disagreed and fought, they also agreed and shared. The joy of being part of a Field where, although they were all creatures and wanted similar things, some chose their leader and some did not. Some creatures spoke languages using their tongues, some their throats and others their noses. Some creatures lived in burrows underground, some in nests on the ground and some lived in hollows in trees. Some creatures ate fish, some berries and nuts, and some herbs and mushrooms. Although each creature was from somewhere and many had moved elsewhere, each of them only had one Field; there was only one place where the creatures could live together. Without the Field, well, there was nothing – just like what lay on the other side of the River. It was nothing because no creature had ever needed to think about it.

Laying together, although far apart, the President and Chair-rabbit felt this thing; this special something with no name. As these thoughts cycled through their minds, the moon peeked from its hiding place behind the horizon to see if it was safe to bravely make its way out into the night sky. At this moment, each leader suddenly felt they might have an idea about what this thing was. Was it God? Was it the thing all creatures knew, called different things and thought was on their side? Was God not a thing like a stone, tree, breeze or a rainstorm? Not a feeling a creature had or something they did? The leaders lay there. The perfect circular form of the moon joined in, beaming at them. Suddenly, they both realised how incredible it was; how incredible that all the creatures in the Field with all their differences managed to live together in one place and mostly get along. Maybe that was God, the special thing that they both felt on the breeze. That thing all creatures felt but could not name and, while they were all different, made them all the same. Maybe God was that thing: the special unspoken understanding every creature in the Field shared.

The two leaders rested a while longer, watching the moon tip-toe its way across the sky, holding paws with each and every star it passed and glowing like a mother holding a newborn carefully in her forepaws.

It was up to them. Perhaps this was the most important moment out of all the moments that there had ever been in the Field. Perhaps they were the most important creatures that had ever lived there. Perhaps it was not and they were not; it did not matter. What mattered was that everything in the Field in this moment depended on them. They grew tired. Across the Field, the last creatures bewitched by the same spell of the night went slowly to their beds.

They got to their paws to follow. How could they do it? They both thought. How could they end all of this? That thing they felt could have been God. That thing that acted both as glue and grease, keeping all the Field's creatures together yet making sure the things they did and wanted carefully slid against each other. It had surrounded them gently and spoken wordlessly. It had told them that they needed to do something different.

As the President climbed the cedar and the Chair-rabbit went down a tunnel into the Warren, although one was going up and the other down, their thoughts met in the middle. They had to agree.

EPILOGUE

And agree they did. The next morning, the Chair-rabbit sent his most trusted ambassador to the Rise to tell the President that the Warren would bring the soldiers and the tongues back from the Pond if the Rise took the tongues back from the Hedgerow and did not give them to more areas. The President did the same, sending his vole ambassador on one final journey back to the Warren to say that the Rise would ask for the tongues back from the Hedgerow and never give them to another area if the Warren took its soldiers and the tongues back from the Pond.

Both ambassadors passed each other on their journeys but neither knew. They passed each other on the way back too, with the same message: both leaders agreed to the other's suggestion.

The President and the Chair-rabbit greeted the news the same way, gently clasping their paws together and shaking them as a smile tickled their exhausted faces. Straight away, both decided that they must meet to add their pawprints to something outlining the things they had agreed. But, to the great annoyance of both leaders, this was difficult. The Prime Minister refused when the President asked the Hedgerow to give the tongues back. And when the Chair-rabbit told the new Chair-frog that the Warren was removing its soldiers from the Pond, he grew upset and threatened to start fighting the Warren. Eventually, as had so often had been the case in the Field, the Rise and Warren agreed to give the Hedgerow and Pond extra food and weapons, offering them protection, no matter what happened. They both accepted.

Both the Rise and Warren went back to the way things were before, and the Chair-rabbit and President never spoke of what happened on that perfect summer's evening to another creature. Neither knew that the other had felt the same thing so they both kept the tongues just in case. Occasionally, when one leader disagreed with the other about something or other, the thought of threatening to use them crossed their minds, but they both knew the power the other held and soon reached an understanding.

Over many seasons, leaders in the Field changed and the older ways creatures organised themselves were steadily replaced by the newer ways of the Rise and Warren. But nothing ever stayed the same for very long in the Field; things were always changing. The spirit of the Rise, rewarding effort and allowing each creature to do whatever they wished slowly became more popular than the Warren's, which encouraged creatures to share everything they collected and made with no creature having the chance to have more things than another. In areas which adopted the ways of the Rise, creatures were encouraged to have different ideas and do what was best for them and their families. In areas which followed the Warren, this did not happen.

All those seasons ago, the rebellious rabbits had underestimated that it was in every creature's nature to want to act for themselves and their families. It was part of the reason why they were creatures, lived, had their own areas and had fought all the fights, dug all the burrows, invaded all the other areas and swapped all the things with each other in the past. They needed to survive, and part of this was acting for themselves, having more food, somewhere to call home and the best weapons to defend it.

In areas that followed the Warren, to make sure creatures did not do this, and did everything for each other instead, the important groups made all the decisions so creatures did not need to, removing the opportunities for them to act only for themselves. To do this, the important groups created other groups for deciding this and that, putting together special armies to keep order and make sure that no creature did anything that was not in the interest of every other creature. But, much like the field mice against the grey squirrels in the Copse, the more the important groups did this, the more unhappy the creatures became. When they became upset, creatures in the Field usually did something about it, starting secret movements or yelling and chanting for change. No matter how much each important group used its army to bring the unhappy creatures back into line, the uprisings continued, much as they had done when the rabbits were unhappy with their old tsar.

Starting with areas furthest away from the Warren, which did not have as much help from the rabbits to stop the uprisings, the soldiers in each of these troubled areas took sides with the unhappy creatures. Gradually, the various groups and the chair-creatures leading them were forced to step aside, leaving each area in turmoil, much as the Pond had been after the frog Emperor's death. One by one the areas changed, the next happening faster than the one before. Where these areas had been reliant on the Warren for help whenever things were not going well, like when they needed more food or creatures were threatening to invade, the Warren was no longer able to do so. It had its own problems; the very same thing was happening there too.

With each uprising and each important group and chair-creature overthrown, one by one the creatures of these areas turned to the Rise. Looking at the areas which organised themselves like the Rise, they were jealous; these areas rarely argued with one another and swapped lots of things backwards and forwards. Having signed the President's agreement all those seasons before, these areas had helped each other rebuild the burrows and nests destroyed during the fighting, and their representatives met regularly in the Brush, making decisions and agreeing on things with all the other areas. The creatures in these areas were free and did what they liked. They had their own ideas and made them happen, just like the shrew brothers had been able to. The more effort they put into collecting and making things, the more food they could have, the bigger the nest or burrow they could build or dig, and the more precious stones and golden nuggets they could gather. The more the uprisings went on, the more these creatures thought being like the

Rise was the thing that would bring peace to their area and make them happy. The Rise, Hedgerow, and all the other areas like them, were only too happy to help.

The unrest in the Warren eventually took its toll there too, yet the rabbits did not turn to the Rise for help straight away. They were proud creatures and, although they did not want to organise themselves the way they had before, they did not want to be like the Rise either, instead trying to sort things out on their own. Before long, only a few areas organised themselves the way the Warren had, but in each, things were a little different. All the frogs in the Pond admired their Chair-frog and could not bear the thought of being without her as their leader. In the Spring, home to the water rats, the Chair-rat was able to keep the creatures there happy by allowing them a little more freedom to have their own things and swap more between themselves, all while keeping the groups for making decisions.

Eventually, though, the Rise won the bloodless fighting with the Warren – the fighting without swords, spears and soldiers, but over which area had the best way of organising themselves and making decisions.

But it was not the end.

The Rise would not be the most important area in the Field forever, nor would the way it did things, which so many areas had copied, be the best way forever.

Nothing stayed the same for very long in the Field; things were always changing. Sometimes they changed slowly, sometimes quickly, but changing they always were. Not all creatures knew this, nor did they know that, while they were all different, they all wanted the same things. They wanted food, they wanted to have families, they wanted to be safe and they wanted to belong and have somewhere to call home. As the Chair-rabbit and President had realised on that summer night all those seasons ago, the most remarkable thing about the Field was not that each one of the different creatures who called it home were able to live there together, but that it even existed at all.